Louisa May Alcott (18
Pennsylvania, and grew
Massachusetts. She receiv
her father, Bronson Alco
as well as from Ralph Waldo Emerson and Henry David
Thoreau, who were family friends. In 1868 she became editor
of the children's magazine *Merry's Museum* and published the
first volume of *Little Women*, a novel about four young sisters
growing up in a small New England town during the Civil
War. *Little Women* was one of the first American novels to
become a classic in children's literature. It remains one of
the best-loved books for girls.

"Recently I revisited *Little Women*, a book I'd read perhaps
three dozen times in childhood. Reading again from a
perspective of adulthood, I saw the profound influence this
book has had on my morals, my values, my longing, and my
dreams. When I stood at Louisa May Alcott's grave in
Concord, Massachusetts, several months ago, I thanked her
again for shaping my thoughts and thus shaping my life."—
Karen Wojahn, as quoted in Kathryn Lindskoog's *Creative
Writing: For People Who Can't Not Write.*

LITTLE WOMEN

Book Two
The Sisters Grow Up

Louisa May Alcott

Edited and abridged
by Kathryn Lindskoog

Illustrated by Barbara Chitouras

MULTNOMAH
Portland, Oregon 97266

Edited by Rodney L. Morris
Illustrations by Barbara Chitouras
Cover design by Durand Demlow

LITTLE WOMEN, BOOK TWO
This abridged edition
© 1991 by Kathryn Lindskoog
Published by Multnomah Press
10209 SE Division Street
Portland, Oregon 97266

Multnomah Press is a ministry of Multnomah School of the Bible, 8435 NE
Glisan Street, Portland, Oregon 97220.

Printed in the United States of America.

Library of Congress Cataloging-in-Publication Data
Lindskoog, Kathryn Ann.
    Little women / Louisa May Alcott : edited and abridged by Kathryn
Lindskoog.
        p.   cm.
        Contents: Bk. 1. Four funny sisters — Bk. 2. The sisters grow up.
        Summary: An abridged retelling of the classic novel, chronicling the
joys and sorrows of the four March sisters as they grow into young ladies
in nineteenth-century New England.
        ISBN 0-88070-437-3 (V. 1) 0-88070-463-2 (V. 2)
        [1. Family life—Fiction. 2. Sisters—Fiction. 3. New England—
Fiction.] I. Alcott, Louisa May, 1832-1888. Little Women. II. Title.
PZ7.L66147Li   1991
[Fic]—dc20   91-27369
                                                                       CIP
                                                                       AC

91 92 93 94 95 96 97 98 - 10 9 8 7 6 5 4 3 2 1

CONTENTS

1
GOSSIP

IN ORDER TO START our story afresh and go to Meg's wedding, we need to begin with a little gossip about the Marches.

The three years that have passed have brought few changes to the quiet family. The war is over, and Mr. March safely at home, busy with his books and the parish where he is a minister. He is rich in the wisdom that is better than learning, the love which calls all mankind "brother." Many admirable people were attracted to him, as sweet herbs draw bees, and he gave them the honey from his fifty years of hard experience. He was young at heart, gentle, and wise.

To outsiders the five energetic women seemed to rule the house, and so they did in many things. But he was still the head of the family, for to him the busy women always turned in troublesome times. He was, in the truest sense of those sacred words, husband and father.

Mrs. March is as brisk and cheery, though grayer, than when we saw her last, and just now absorbed in Meg's affairs.

John Brooke was in the army for a year, got wounded, was sent home, and not allowed to return. He received no stars or bars, but he deserved them. He devoted himself to getting well, preparing for business, and earning a home for Meg. With good sense and sturdy independence, he refused Mr. Laurence's generous offers, and became a bookkeeper, preferring an honestly earned salary to running any risks with borrowed money.

Meg was prettier than ever, for love is a great beautifier. Ned Moffat had just married Sallie Gardiner, and Meg couldn't help contrasting their fine house and carriage and many gifts with her own, secretly wishing she could have the same. But envy vanished when she thought of all the patient love and labor John had put into the little home awaiting her, and when they sat together in the twilight, talking over their small plans, the future always grew so beautiful and bright that she forgot Sallie's splendor, and felt herself the richest, happiest girl in Christendom.

Jo never went back to Aunt March, for the old lady took such a fancy to Amy that she bribed her with the offer of drawing lessons from one of the best teachers going. So Amy gave her mornings to duty and her afternoons to pleasure. Jo meantime devoted herself to writing and to Beth, who remained delicate long after scarlet fever was a thing of the past. Not an invalid exactly, but never again the rosy, healthy creature she had been, yet always hopeful, happy, and serene, busy with the quiet duties she loved, everyone's friend, and an angel in the house.

As long as *The Spread Eagle* paid her a dollar a column for her "rubbish," as she called it, Jo felt herself a woman of means, and spun her little romances diligently. But great plans fermented in her busy brain, and the old tin box in the garret held a slowly increasing pile of blotted manuscript, which was one day to place the name of March upon the roll of fame.

Laurie, having gone to college to please his grandfather, was now getting through it in the easiest possible manner. Thanks to money, manners, much talent, and the kindest heart that ever got its owner into scrapes by trying to get other people out of them, he stood in great danger of being spoiled by popularity. He probably would have been had he not possessed armor against evil: his memory of the kind old man bound up in his success; the friend who watched over him as if he were her son; and the knowledge that four girls loved, admired, and believed in him with all their hearts.

High spirits and the love of fun caused many college pranks. He prided himself on his narrow escapes, and liked to thrill the girls with graphic accounts of his triumphs over wrathful tutors, dignified professors, and vanquished enemies. The "men of my class" were heroes in the eyes of the girls, who were frequently allowed to bask in the smiles of these great creatures, when Laurie brought them home with him.

Amy especially enjoyed this high honor, and became quite a belle among them. Meg was too much absorbed in John to care for any other lords of creation, and Beth too shy to do more than peep at them and wonder how Amy dared to order them about so. But Jo felt in her element, and found it difficult to refrain from imitating the gentlemanly attitudes and phrases which seemed more natural to her than the decorums prescribed for young ladies. They all liked Jo immensely, but never fell in love with her, though few escaped without paying the tribute of a sentimental sigh or two at Amy's shrine. And speaking of sentiment brings us naturally to the "Dovecote."

That was the name of the little brown house which Mr. Brooke had prepared for Meg's first home. Laurie had christened it, saying it was highly appropriate to the gentle lovers who "went on together like a pair of turtledoves, with first a bill and then a coo." It was a tiny house, with a little garden behind and a lawn about as big as a pocket handkerchief in front. Here Meg meant to have a fountain, shrubbery, and a profusion of lovely flowers; though just at present the fountain was represented by a weather-beaten urn, like a dilapidated slopbowl, the shrubbery consisted of several young larches, undecided whether to live or die, and the profusion of flowers was merely hinted by regiments of sticks to show where seeds were planted.

But inside, it was altogether charming. To be sure, the hall was narrow, the dining room was so small that six people were a tight fit, and the kitchen stairs seemed built for the express purpose of dropping both servants and china pell-mell into the coalbin. But they got used to these slight blemishes. There were no marble-topped tables, long mirrors, or lace curtains in the little parlor, but simple furniture, plenty of books, a fine picture or two, flowers in the bay window, and, scattered all about, pretty gifts from friends.

No storeroom was ever better provided with good wishes, merry words, and happy hopes than that in which Jo and her mother put away Meg's few boxes, barrels, and bundles. The kitchen never could have looked so cozy and neat if Hannah had not arranged every pot and pan a dozen times over, and laid the fire all ready for lighting. I also doubt if any young housewife ever began life with so rich a supply of dusters and potholders, for Beth made enough to last till the silver wedding came round, and invented three different kinds of dishcloths for the bridal china.

People who hire all these things done for them never know what they lose, for the homeliest tasks get beautified if loving hands do them.

In his love of jokes, Laurie, though nearly through college, was as much of a boy as ever. His last whim had been to bring with him on his weekly visits some new, useful, and ingenious article for the young housekeeper. Now a bag of remarkable clothespins; next, a wonderful nutmeg grater which fell to pieces at the first trial; a knife cleaner that spoiled all the knives; or a sweeper that picked the nap neatly off the carpet and left the dirt; laborsaving soap that took the skin off one's hands; infallible glues that stuck firmly to nothing but fingers; and every kind of tinware, from a toy savings bank for odd pennies to a wonderful boiler which would wash articles in its own steam with every prospect of exploding in the process.

Everything was done at last, even to Amy's arranging different colored soaps to match the different colored rooms, and Beth's setting the table for the first meal.

"Are you satisfied? Does it seem like home, and do you feel as if you should be happy here?" asked Mrs. March, as she and her daughter went through the new kingdom arm in arm, for just then they seemed to cling together more tenderly than ever.

"Yes, Mother, perfectly satisfied, thanks to you all, and so happy that I can't talk about it," answered Meg, with a look that was better than words.

"If she only had a servant or two it would be all right," said Amy, coming out of the parlor, where she had been trying to decide whether the bronze Mercury looked best on the whatnot or the mantelpiece.

"Mother and I have talked that over. There will be so little to do that with Lotty to run my errands and help me here and there, I shall only have enough work to keep me from getting lazy or homesick," answered Meg tranquilly.

"Sallie Moffat has four," began Amy.

"If Meg had four the house wouldn't hold them, and Mr. and Mrs. would have to camp in the garden," broke in Jo, who, enveloped in a big blue pinafore, was giving the last polish to the door handles.

"Meg and John begin humbly," said Mother, "but I have a feeling that there will be as much happiness in the little house as in the big one. When I was first married, I used to long for my new clothes to wear out or get torn, so that I might have the pleasure of mending them, for I got heartily sick of doing fancywork and tending my pocket handkerchief."

"Why didn't you go into the kitchen and make messes, as Sallie says she does to amuse herself, though they never turn out well and the servants laugh at her," said Meg.

"I did after a while, to learn of Hannah how things should be done. It was play then, but there came a time when I was truly grateful that I possessed the power to cook wholesome food for my little girls, and help myself when I could no longer afford to hire help. You begin at the other end, Meg, dear, but the lessons you learn now will be of use to you by-and-by when John is a richer man, for the mistress of a house, however splendid, should know how work ought to be done."

"Yes, Mother, I'm sure of that," said Meg, listening respectfully to the little lecture, for the best of women will hold forth upon the all-absorbing subject of housekeeping. "Do you know I like this room most," added Meg, a minute after, as they went upstairs and she looked into her well-stored linen closet.

Beth was there, laying the snowy piles smoothly on the shelves. All three laughed as Meg spoke, for that linen closet was a joke. You see, having said that if Meg married "that Brooke" she shouldn't have a cent of her money, Aunt March was in a quandary when time had made her repent her vow. She never broke her word, and at last devised a plan. Mrs Carrol, Florence's mamma, was ordered to buy a generous supply of linens and send it as a present. The secret leaked out and was greatly enjoyed by the family, for Aunt March insisted she could give nothing but the old-fashioned pearls long promised to the first bride.

"Toodles is coming," cried Jo from below, and they all went down to meet Laurie, whose weekly visit was an important event in their quiet lives.

A tall, broad-shouldered young fellow, with a cropped head, a felt basin of a hat, and a flyaway coat, came tramping down the road at a great pace, walked over the low fence without stopping to open the gate, straight up to Mrs. March, with both hands out and a hearty—"Here I am, Mother! Everything's all right."

The last words were in answer to her kindly questioning look which the handsome eyes met so frankly that the little ceremony closed, as usual, with a motherly kiss.

"For Mrs. John Brooke, with the maker's congratulations and compliments. Bless you, Beth! What a refreshing spectacle you are, Jo. Amy, you are getting altogether too handsome for a single lady."

As Laurie spoke, he delivered a brown-paper parcel to Meg, pulled Beth's hair ribbon, stared at Jo's big pinafore, and fell into an attitude of mock rapture before Amy, then shook hands all round, and everyone began to talk.

"Where is John?" asked Meg anxiously.

"Stopped to get the license for tomorrow, ma'am."

"Which side won the last match, Teddy?" inquired Jo.

"Ours, of course. Wish you'd been there to see."

"How is the lovely Miss Randal?" asked Amy with a significant smile.

"More cruel than ever. Don't you see how I'm pining away?" And Laurie gave his broad chest a sounding slap and heaved a melodramatic sigh.

"What's the last joke? Undo the bundle and see, Meg," said Beth, eyeing the knobby parcel with curiosity.

"It's a useful thing to have in the house in case of fire or thieves," observed Laurie, as a watchman's rattle appeared, amid the laughter of the girls.

"Any time when John is away and you get frightened, Mrs. Meg, just swing that out of the front window, and it will rouse the neighborhood in a jiffy. Nice thing, isn't it?" And Laurie gave them a sample of its powers that made them cover their ears.

"There's gratitude for you! And speaking of gratitude reminds me to mention that you may thank Hannah for saving your wedding cake from destruction. I saw it going into your house as I came by, and if she hadn't defended it manfully I'd have had a pick at it, for it looked like a remarkably plummy one."

"I wonder if you will ever grow up, Laurie," said Meg in a matronly tone.

"I'm doing my best, ma'am, but can't get much higher, I'm afraid, as six feet is about all men can do in these degenerate days," responded the young gentleman, whose head was about level with the little chandelier. "As I'm tremendously hungry, I propose an adjournment."

"Mother and I are going to wait for John. There are some last things to settle," said Meg, bustling away.

"Beth and I are going over to Kitty Bryant's to get more flowers for tomorrow," added Amy, tying a picturesque hat over her picturesque curls, and enjoying the effect as much as anybody.

"Come, Jo, don't desert a fellow. I'm in such a state of exhaustion I can't get home without help. Don't take off your apron, whatever you do; it's peculiarly becoming," said Laurie, as Jo offered him her arm to support his feeble steps.

"Now, Teddy, I want to talk seriously to you about tomorrow," began Jo, as they strolled away together. "You must promise to behave well, and not cut up any pranks and spoil our plans."

"Not a prank."

"And don't say funny things when we ought to be sober."

"I never do. You are the one for that."

"And I implore you not to look at me during the ceremony. I shall certainly laugh if you do."

"You won't see me, you'll be crying so hard that the thick fog round you will obscure the view."

"I never cry unless for some great affliction."

"Such as fellows going to college, hey?" cut in Laurie, with a suggestive laugh.

"Don't be a peacock. I only moaned a trifle to keep the girls company."

"Exactly. I say, Jo, how is Grandpa this week? Pretty amiable?"

"Very. Why, have you got into a scrape and want to know how he'll take it?" asked Jo rather sharply.

"Now, Jo, do you think I'd look your mother in the face and say 'All right,' if it wasn't?" And Laurie stopped short, with an injured air.

"No, I don't."

"Then don't go and be suspicious. I only want some money," said Laurie, walking on again, appeased by her hearty tone.

"You spend a great deal, Teddy."

"Bless you, I don't spend it, it spends itself somehow, and is gone before I know it."

"You are so generous and kindhearted that you let people borrow, and can't say 'No' to anyone. We heard about Henshaw and all you did for him. If you always spent money in that way, no one would blame you," said Jo warmly.

"Oh, he made a mountain out of a molehill. You wouldn't have me let that fine fellow work himself to death just for the want of a little help, when he is worth a dozen of us lazy chaps, would you?"

"Of course not, but I don't see the use of your having seventeen waistcoats, endless neckties, and a new hat every time you come home. I thought you'd got over the dandy period, but every now and then it breaks out in a new spot. Just now it's the fashion to be hideous—to make your head look like a scrubbing brush, wear a tight jacket, orange gloves, and clumping square-toed boots. If it was cheap ugliness, I'd say nothing, but it costs as much as the other, and I don't get any satisfaction out of it."

Laurie threw back his head and laughed so heartily at this attack, that the felt hat fell off, and Jo walked on it. He folded up the maltreated hat and stuffed it into his pocket.

"Don't lecture any more, there's a good soul!" Laurie said. "I have enough all through the week, and like to enjoy myself when I come home."

"I'll leave you in peace if you'll only let your hair grow," observed Jo severely.

"This unassuming style promotes study, that's why we adopt it," returned Laurie, who certainly could not be accused of vanity, having voluntarily sacrificed a handsome curly crop to the demand for quarter-of-an-inch-long stubble.

"By the way, Jo, I think that little Parker is really getting desperate about Amy. He talks of her constantly, writes poetry, and moons about. He'd better nip his little passion in the bud, hadn't he?" added

Laurie, in a confidential, elder-brotherly tone, after a minute's silence.

"Of course he had. We don't want any more marrying in this family for years to come. Mercy on us, what are the children thinking of?" And Jo looked as much scandalized as if Amy and little Parker were not yet in their teens.

"It's a fast age, and I don't know what we are coming to, ma'am. You are a mere infant, but you'll go next, Jo, and we'll be left lamenting," said Laurie, shaking his head over the degeneracy of the times.

"Don't be alarmed. I'm not one of the agreeable sort. Nobody will want me, and it's a mercy, for there should always be one old maid in a family."

"You won't give anyone a chance," said Laurie, with a sidelong glance and a little more color than before in his sunburned face. "You won't show the soft side of your character, and if a fellow gets a peep at it by accident and can't help showing that he likes it, you throw cold water over him."

"I don't like that sort of thing, I'm too busy to be worried with nonsense, and I think it's dreadful to break up families so. I don't wish to get cross, so let's change the subject." And Jo looked ready to fling cold water on the slightest provocation.

Whatever his feelings might have been, Laurie found a vent for them in a long low whistle and the fearful prediction as they parted at the gate, "Mark my words, Jo, you'll go next."

2

THE FIRST WEDDING

THE JUNE ROSES OVER THE PORCH were awake bright and early on that morning, rejoicing in the cloudless sunshine. They swung in the wind, whispering to one another, for some peeped in at the dining-room windows where the feast was spread, some climbed up to nod and smile at the sisters as they dressed the bride, others waved a welcome to those who came and went on various errands, and all, from the rosiest full-blown flower to the palest baby bud, offered their beauty and fragrance to Meg, who had loved and tended them so long.

Meg looked like a rose herself, for all that was best and sweetest in heart and soul seemed to bloom in her face that day. Neither silk, lace, nor orange blossoms would she have. "I don't want to look strange or fixed up today," she said. "I don't want a fashionable wedding, but only those about me whom I love, and to them I wish to look and be my familiar self."

So she made her wedding gown herself, sewing into it the tender hopes and innocent romances of a girlish heart. Her sisters braided up her pretty hair, and the only ornaments she wore were the lilies of the valley, which "her John" liked best of all the flowers that grew.

"You do look just like our own dear Meg, only so sweet and lovely that I should hug you if it wouldn't crumple your dress," cried Amy.

"Then I am satisfied. But please hug and kiss me, everyone, and don't mind my dress. I want a great many crumples of this sort put into it today."

Meg opened her arms to her sisters, who clung about her for a minute, feeling that the new love had not changed the old.

"Now I'm going to tie John's cravat for him, and then stay a few minutes with Father quietly in the study." And Meg ran down to perform these little ceremonies. This may be a good time to tell of a few changes which three years have made in the appearance of the younger girls, for all are looking their best just now.

Jo has learned to carry herself with ease, if not grace. Her curly bob has lengthened into a thick coil, more becoming to the small head atop the tall figure. There is a fresh color in her brown cheeks, a soft shine in her eyes, and only gentle words fall from her sharp tongue today.

Beth has grown slender, pale, and more quiet than ever. The beautiful, kind eyes are larger, and in them lies an expression that saddens one, although it is not sad itself. It is the shadow of pain, but Beth seldom complains and always speaks hopefully of "being better soon."

Amy is considered "the flower of the family," for at sixteen she has indescribable charm. One saw it in the motion of her hands, the flow of her dress. Amy's nose still afflicted her, and so did her mouth, being too wide. These features gave character to her whole face, but she never could see it, and consoled herself with her wonderful complexion, keen blue eyes, and curls more golden and abundant than ever.

All three wore suits of thin silver gray (their best gowns for the summer), with blush roses in hair and bosom. All three looked just what they were—fresh-faced, happy-hearted girls, pausing a moment in their busy lives to read with wistful eyes the sweetest chapter in the romance of womanhood.

There was to be no formality; everything was to be as natural and

Meg opened her arms to her sisters, who clung about her for a minute, feeling that the new love had not changed the old.

19

homelike as possible. So when Aunt March arrived, she was scandalized to see the bride come running to welcome and lead her in, and to find the bridegroom fastening up a garland that had fallen down.

"Upon my word, here's a state of things!" cried the old lady, taking the seat of honor prepared for her, and settling the folds of her lavender silk with a great rustle. "You oughtn't to be seen till the last minute, child."

"I'm not a show, Aunty, and no one is coming to stare at me, to criticize my dress, or count the cost of my luncheon. I'm too happy to care what anyone says or thinks, and I'm going to have my little wedding just as I like it. John, dear, here's your hammer."

Mr. Brooke didn't even say, "Thank you," but as he stooped for the unromantic tool, he kissed his little bride with a look that made Aunt March whisk out her pocket handkerchief with a sudden dew in her sharp old eyes.

A crash, a cry, and a laugh from Laurie, "Jo's upset the cake again!" caused a momentary flurry, which was hardly over when a flock of cousins arrived.

"Don't let that young giant come near me, he worries me worse than mosquitoes," whispered the old lady to Amy, as the rooms filled and Laurie's black head towered above the rest.

"He has promised to be good today, and he can be perfectly elegant if he likes," returned Amy, gliding away to warn him, which caused him to haunt the old lady with a devotion that nearly distracted her.

There was no bridal procession, but a sudden silence fell upon the room as Mr. March and the young pair took their places under the green arch. Mother and sisters gathered close; the fatherly voice broke more than once, which only seemed to make the service more beautiful and solemn. The bridegroom's hand trembled visibly, and no one heard his replies. But Meg looked straight up in her husband's eyes, and said, "I will!" with such tender trust in her own face and voice that her mother's heart rejoiced and Aunt March sniffed audibly.

Jo did not cry, though she was near it once, and was only saved from a demonstration by the consciousness that Laurie was staring fixedly at her, with a comical mixture of merriment and emotion in his wicked black eyes. Beth kept her face hidden on her mother's shoulder, but Amy stood like a graceful statue, with a most becoming ray of sunshine touching her white forehead and the flower in her hair.

The minute Meg was fairly married, she cried, "The first kiss for Marmee!" During the next fifteen minutes she looked more like a rose than ever, for everyone kissed her, from Mr. Laurence to old Hannah, who hugged her in the hall, crying with a sob and a chuckle, "Bless you, deary, a hundred times! The cake ain't hurt a mite, and everything looks lovely."

Everybody said something brilliant, or tried to, which did just as well, for laughter is ready when hearts are light. There was no display of gifts, for they were already in the little house, nor was there an elaborate meal, but a lunch of cake and fruit, trimmed with flowers. Mr. Laurence and Aunt March shrugged and smiled at one another when water, lemonade, and coffee were found to be the only drinks. No one said anything, however, till Laurie, who insisted on serving the bride, appeared before her with a loaded tray in his hand and a puzzled expression on his face.

"Has Jo smashed all the bottles by accident," he whispered, "or am I merely laboring under a delusion that I saw some here this morning?"

"No, your grandfather kindly offered us his best, and Aunt March actually sent some, but Father sent it on to the Soldiers' Home. You know he thinks that wine should be used only in illness, and Mother says that neither she nor her daughters will ever offer it to any young man under her roof."

Meg expected to see Laurie frown or laugh, but he did neither, for after a quick look at her, he said, in his impetuous way, "I like that! For I've seen enough harm done to wish other women would think as you do."

"You are not made wise by experience, I hope?" And there was an anxious accent in Meg's voice.

"No, I give you my word for it. This is not one of my temptations. Being brought up where wine is as common as water and almost as harmless, I don't care for it—but when a pretty girl offers it, one doesn't like to refuse, you see."

"But you should, for the sake of others, if not for your own. Come, Laurie, promise, and give me one more reason to call this the happiest day of my life."

A demand so sudden and so serious made the young man hesitate a moment. Meg knew that if he gave the promise he would keep it at all costs. She did not speak, but she looked up at him with a face made eloquent by happiness, and a smile which said, "No one can refuse me anything today."

Laurie certainly could not, and with an answering smile, he gave her his hand, saying heartily, "I promise, Mrs. Brooke!"

"I thank you, very, very much."

"And I drink 'long life to your resolution,' Teddy," cried Jo, as she waved her glass of lemonade and beamed approvingly upon him.

So the toast was drunk, the pledge made and loyally kept in spite of many temptations, for the girls had seized a happy moment to do their friend a favor for which he thanked them all his life.

After lunch, people strolled about, by twos and threes, through house and garden, enjoying the sunshine without and within. Meg and John happened to be standing together in the middle of the lawn, when Laurie was seized with an inspiration which put the finishing touch to this unfashionable wedding.

"All the married people take hands and dance round the new-made husband and wife, while we bachelors and spinsters prance in couples outside the circle!" cried Laurie. The young folks flittered through the garden like butterflies on a midsummer day. Lack of breath brought the impromptu ball to a close, and then people began to go.

"I wish you well, my dear, I heartily wish you well. But I think you'll be sorry for it," said Aunt March to Meg, adding to the bridegroom, as he led her to the carriage, "You've got a treasure, young man. See that you deserve it."

"That is the prettiest wedding I've been to for an age, Ned, and I don't see why, for there wasn't a bit of style about it," observed Mrs. Moffat to her husband, as they drove away.

"Laurie, my lad, if you ever want to indulge in this sort of thing, get one of those little girls to help you, and I shall be perfectly satisfied," said Mr. Laurence, settling himself in his easy chair to rest.

"I'll do my best to gratify you, sir," was Laurie's unusually dutiful reply, as he carefully unpinned the posy Jo had put in his buttonhole.

The little house was not far away, and the only bridal journey Meg had was the quiet walk with John from the old home to the new. When she came down, looking like a pretty Quaker in her dove-colored suit and straw bonnet tied with white, they all gathered about her to say goodbye, as tenderly as if she had been going on the grand tour of Europe.

"Don't feel that I am separated from you, Marmee dear, or that I love you any less for loving John so much," she said, clinging to her mother, with full eyes for a moment. "I shall come every day, Father, and expect to keep my old place in all your hearts, though I am married. Beth is going to be with me a great deal, and the other girls will drop in now and then to laugh at my housekeeping struggles. Thank you all for my happy wedding day. Goodbye, goodbye!"

They stood watching her, with faces full of love and hope and tender pride as she walked away, leaning on her husband's arm, with her hands full of flowers and the June sunshine brightening her happy face. And so Meg's married life began.

3

ARTISTIC ATTEMPTS

IT TAKES PEOPLE A LONG TIME to learn the difference between talent and genius, especially ambitious young men and women. Mistaking enthusiasm for inspiration, Amy attempted every branch of art. She devoted herself to pen-and-ink drawing, in which she showed taste and skill. But overstrained eyes soon caused pen and ink to be laid aside for a bold attempt at burning designs on wood with a hot poker. While this attack lasted, the family lived in constant fear of a fire.

From fire to oil was a natural transition for burned fingers, and Amy turned to painting. An artist friend gave her his castoff palettes, brushes, and colors, and she daubed away, producing landscapes and seascapes such as were never seen on land or sea. She painted tempests of blue thunder, orange lightning, brown rain, and purple clouds, with a tomato colored splash in the middle, which might be seen as the sun, a sailor's shirt, or a king's robe.

Charcoal portraits came next, and the entire family hung in a row, looking as if they climbed out of a coalbin. Softened into crayon sketches, they did better, for the likenesses were good, and Amy's hair, Jo's nose, Meg's mouth, and Laurie's eyes were pronounced "wonderfully fine." A return to clay and plaster followed. She undertook to cast her own pretty foot, and the family was one day alarmed by an unearthly bumping and screaming—and running to the rescue, found the young enthusiast hopping wildly about the shed with her foot held fast in a pan full of plaster, which had hardened with unexpected rapidity.

After this, a mania for sketching from nature set her to haunting river, field, and wood. She caught endless colds sitting on damp grass, and got a wrinkle over her nose from squinting at light and shade. She persevered in spite of all obstacles, failures, and discouragements, firmly believing that in time she should do something worthy to be called "high art."

She had resolved to be an attractive and accomplished woman, even if she never became a great artist, and here she succeeded better. She had an instinctive sense of what was pleasing and proper, always said the right thing to the right person, did just what suited the time and place, and was so self-possessed that her sisters used to say, "If Amy went to court without any rehearsal beforehand, she'd know exactly what to do."

Money, position, fashionable accomplishments, and elegant manners were most desirable in her eyes, and she liked to associate with those who possessed them, often mistaking the false for the true, and admiring what was not admirable. She cultivated her aristocratic tastes and feelings, so that when opportunity came she might be ready.

"My lady," as her friends called her, sincerely desired to be a genuine lady, and was so at heart, but had yet to learn that money cannot buy refinement of nature, that rank does not always confer nobility, and that true breeding makes itself felt in spite of external drawbacks.

"I want to ask a favor of you, Mamma," Amy said, coming in with an important air one day. "Our drawing class breaks up next week, and before the girls separate for the summer, I want to ask them out here for a day. They are wild to see the river, sketch the broken bridge, and copy some of the things they admire in my sketchbook. They are all rich and know I am poor, yet they don't treat me differently."

"Why should they?" asked Mrs. March.

"You know as well as I that it does make a difference with nearly everyone, so don't ruffle up like a dear mother hen. The ugly duckling turned out a swan, you know." And Amy smiled, for she possessed a happy temper and hopeful spirit.

Mrs. March laughed and smoothed down her maternal pride as she asked, "Well, my swan, what is your plan?"

"I should like to ask the girls here to lunch next week, take them to the places they want to see, a row on the river, perhaps, and make a little party for them."

"That looks feasible. What do you want for lunch? Cake, sandwiches, fruit, and coffee will be all that is necessary, I suppose?"

"Oh dear, no! We must have cold tongue and chicken, French chocolate and ice cream. The girls are used to such things, and I want my lunch to be proper and elegant, though I do work for my living."

"How many young ladies are there?" asked her mother, beginning to look sober.

"Twelve or fourteen in the class, but I dare say they won't all come."

"All this will be expensive, Amy."

"Not very. I've calculated the cost, and I'll pay for it myself."

"Don't you think, dear, that some simpler plan would be more pleasant to them, as a change if nothing more, and much better for us?"

"If I can't have it as I like, I don't care to have it at all. I know that I can carry it out perfectly well, if you and the girls will help a little, and I don't see why I can't if I'm willing to pay for it," said Amy.

Mrs. March knew that experience was an excellent teacher when her children objected to taking advice. "Very well, Amy, if your heart is set upon it, and you see your way through without too great an outlay of money, time, and temper, I'll do my best to help you."

"Thanks, Mother, you are always so kind." And away went Amy to lay her plan before her sisters.

Meg agreed at once, but Jo frowned upon the whole project. "Why in the world should you spend your money, worry your family, and turn the house upside down for a parcel of girls who don't care a sixpence for you? I thought you had too much pride and sense to truckle to anyone," said Jo, who, being called from the tragic climax of her novel, was not in the best mood for social enterprises.

"I don't truckle!" returned Amy indignantly. "The girls do care for me, and I for them, and there's a great deal of kindness and sense and talent among them, in spite of what you call fashionable nonsense. You don't care to make people like you, to go into good society, and cultivate your manners and tastes, but I do. You can go through life with your elbows out and your nose in the air and call it independence, if you like. That's not my way."

Amy seldom failed to have common sense on her side, and her definition of Jo's idea of independence was such a good hit that both burst out laughing. Much against her will, Jo at length consented to sacrifice a day to help her sister through "a nonsensical business."

The invitations were sent, nearly all accepted, and the following Monday was set apart for the grand event. Having made up her mind what to do, Amy proceeded to do it in spite of all obstacles. To begin with, Hannah's cooking didn't turn out well: the chicken was tough, the tongue too salty, and the chocolate wouldn't froth properly. Then the cake and ice cream cost more than Amy expected, and various other expenses, which seemed trifling at the outset, counted up alarmingly. Beth caught cold and took to her bed, Meg had an unusual number of callers to keep her at home, and Jo's accidents and mistakes were uncommonly numerous.

"If it hadn't been for Mother I never would have gotten through," Amy declared afterward.

If it was not good weather on Monday, the young ladies were to come on Tuesday—an arrangement which frustrated Jo and Hannah. On Monday morning the weather was in that undecided state which is more exasperating than a steady pour. It drizzled a little, shone a little, blew a little, and didn't make up its mind till it was too late for anyone else to make up theirs.

Amy was up at dawn, hustling people out of their beds and through their breakfasts. The parlor struck her as looking uncommonly shabby, but she skillfully made the best of what she had, arranging chairs over the worn places in the carpet, covering stains on the walls with pictures framed in ivy, and filling up empty corners with homemade statuary and the lovely vases of flowers Jo scattered about. The lunch looked charming, and as she surveyed it, Amy sincerely hoped it would taste good, and that the borrowed glass, china, and silver would get safely home again.

Then came two hours of suspense, during which she vibrated from parlor to porch. A shower at eleven had evidently quenched the enthusiasm of the young ladies who were to arrive at noon, for nobody came. At two the exhausted family sat down in a blaze of sunshine to consume the perishable portions of the feast, that nothing might be wasted.

As the sun woke her next morning, Amy said, "No doubt about the weather today. They will certainly come, so we must fly round and be ready for them." She spoke briskly, but in her secret soul she wished she had said nothing about Tuesday, for her interest—like her cake— was getting a little stale.

"I can't get any lobsters, so you will have to do without lobster salad today," said Mr. March, coming from the local shop.

"Use the chicken then, the toughness won't matter in a salad," advised Mrs. March.

"Hannah left the chicken on the kitchen table a minute, and the kittens got at it. I'm very sorry, Amy," added Beth.

"Then I must have a lobster," said Amy decidedly.

"Shall I rush into town and demand one?" asked Jo, like a martyr.

"I'll go myself," answered Amy, whose temper was beginning to fail.

Wearing a thick veil and armed with a covered basket, she departed, feeling that a cool ride in the public carriage would soothe her ruffled spirit. After some delay, the live lobster was procured, likewise a bottle of salad dressing to save time at home, and off she rode again.

Since the carriage contained only a sleepy old lady, Amy pocketed her veil and began trying to find out where all her money had gone. So busy was she with her figuring that she did not observe a newcomer, till a masculine voice said, "Good morning, Miss March," and, looking up, she beheld one of Laurie's most elegant college friends.

They got on excellently, and she was chatting away in a peculiarly lofty strain, when the old lady got out. In stumbling to the door, she upset the basket, and—oh, horror!—the huge lobster appeared.

"By Jove, she's forgotten her dinner!" cried the young man, poking the scarlet monster into its place with his cane, and preparing to hand out the basket after the old lady.

"Please don't . . . it's . . . it's mine," murmured Amy, with a face nearly as red as her lobster.

"Oh, really, I beg pardon. It's an uncommonly fine one, isn't it?" he said gallantly.

Amy recovered herself in a breath, set her basket boldly on the seat, and said, laughing, "Don't you wish you were to have some of the salad he's going to make, and to see the charming young ladies who are to eat it?"

That made her feel less ridiculous. "I suppose he'll laugh and joke over it with Laurie, but I shan't see them, that's a comfort," thought Amy, as the young man bowed and departed.

She did not mention the upset at home (though she discovered that her new dress was much damaged by the rivulets of dressing that meandered down the skirt), but went through with the preparations which now seemed more irksome than before, and at twelve o'clock all was ready again. She wished to efface the memory of yesterday's failure by a grand success today; so she ordered the carriage they had borrowed from Mr. Laurence and drove away to meet and escort her guests to the banquet.

"They're coming! I'll go onto the porch to meet them," said Mrs. March. But after one glance, she returned with an indescribable expression—for, looking quite lost in the big carriage, sat Amy and one young lady.

"Run, Beth, and help Hannah clear half the things off the table. It will be too absurd to put a luncheon for twelve before a single girl," cried Jo.

In came Amy, calm and delightfully cordial to the one guest who had kept her promise. The rest of the family played their parts equally well. The remodeled lunch being gaily partaken of, the studio and garden visited, and art discussed with enthusiasm, Amy ordered a small buggy and drove her friend quietly about the neighborhood till sunset.

As she came walking in, looking tired but as composed as ever, she observed that every vestige of the unfortunate party had disappeared, except a suspicious pucker about the corners of Jo's mouth.

"You've had a lovely afternoon for your drive, dear," said her mother, as respectfully as if the whole twelve had come.

"Miss Eliott is a sweet girl, and seemed to enjoy herself, I thought," observed Beth, with unusual warmth.

"Could you spare me some of your cake? I really need some, I have so much company, and I can't make such delicious stuff as yours," asked Meg soberly.

"Take it all. I'm the only one here who likes sweet things, and it will mold before I can dispose of it," answered Amy, thinking of all the waste.

"It's a pity Laurie isn't here to help us," began Jo, as they sat down to ice cream and lobster salad for the second time in two days.

The whole family ate in heroic silence, till Mr. March mildly observed, "Salad was one of the favorite dishes of the ancients . . ."

Here a general explosion of laughter cut short his history lesson.

"Bundle everything into a basket and send it to the Hummels. I'm sick of the sight of this, and there's no reason you should all die from overeating because I've been a fool," cried Amy, wiping her eyes.

"I thought I should have died when I saw you two girls rattling about in the carriage, and Mother waiting in state to receive the throng," sighed Jo, spent with laughter.

"I'm sorry you were disappointed, dear, but we all did our best," said Mrs. March, in a tone full of motherly regret.

"I am satisfied; it's not my fault that it failed," said Amy, with a little quiver in her voice. "I thank you all for helping me, and I'll thank you still more if you won't refer to it for a month, at least."

No one did for several months, but Laurie's birthday gift to Amy was a charm in the shape of a tiny coral lobster.

4
LITERARY LESSONS

FORTUNE SUDDENLY SMILED UPON JO, and dropped a good-luck penny in her path. Not a golden penny, exactly, but it gave her more real happiness.

Every few weeks she would shut herself up in her room, put on her scribbling suit, and write away at her novel with all her heart and soul, for till that was finished she could find no peace. Her "scribbling suit" consisted of a black woolen pinafore on which she could wipe her inky pen, and a cap of the same material, adorned with a cheerful red bow, into which she bundled her hair when the decks were cleared for action. If this hat was drawn low upon the forehead, it was a sign that hard work was going on, in exciting moments it was pushed rakishly askew, and when despair seized the author it was plucked wholly off, and cast upon the floor. Not until the red bow was gaily erect did anyone dare speak to Jo.

One week Jo agreed to escort Miss Crocker to a lecture on the Pyramids, and Jo took it for granted that some great social evil would be remedied or some great want supplied by unfolding the glories of the Pharaohs to an audience whose thoughts were busy with the price of coal and flour, and whose lives were spent in trying to solve harder riddles than that of the Sphinx.

They were early, and Jo amused herself by examining the faces of the people who occupied the row with them. On her left were two matrons, with massive foreheads and bonnets to match, discussing Women's Rights and making tatting. Beyond sat a pair of humble lovers holding each other by the hand, a spinster eating peppermints out of a paper bag, and an old gentleman napping behind a yellow bandanna. On her right, her only neighbor was a studious-looking lad absorbed in a newspaper.

It was a fiction tabloid, and Jo idly wondered about the melodramatic illustration of an Indian in full war costume, tumbling over a precipice with a wolf at his throat, while two infuriated young gentlemen with unnaturally small feet and big eyes, were stabbing each other close by, and a disheveled female was flying away in the background with her mouth wide open. Pausing to turn a page, the lad saw her looking and offered half his paper, saying, "Want to read it? That's a first-rate story."

Jo accepted it with a smile, for she had never outgrown her liking for boys, and soon found herself involved in a story of love, mystery, and murder, in which the passions run wild, and when the author's invention fails, a grand catastrophe clears the stage of one half the characters.

"Prime, isn't it?" asked the boy.

"I think you and I could do as well as that if we tried," returned Jo, amused at his admiration of the trash.

"I should think I was a pretty lucky chap if I could. I read all her pieces, and I know a fellow who works in the office where this paper is printed. She knows just what folks like, and gets paid well for writing it."

Here the lecture began, but Jo heard little of it, for while Professor Sands was talking about Cheops and hieroglyphics, she was taking down the address of the paper, and boldly resolving to try for the hundred-dollar prize offered in its columns for a sensational story. By the time the lecture ended and the audience awoke, she was already deep in her story, unable to decide whether the duel should come before the elopement or after the murder.

She said nothing of her plan at home, but fell to work the next day. She had contented herself until now with mild romances for *The Spread Eagle*, but her home theater and constant reading supplied her with a sense of dramatic action, plot, language, and costumes. Her story was as full of desperation and despair as her limited acquaintance with those uncomfortable emotions enabled her to make it, and, having located it in Lisbon, she wound up with an earthquake. She sent the manuscript with a note, modestly saying that if the tale didn't get the prize, which the writer hardly dared expect, she would be glad to receive any sum at all.

Six weeks is a long time to wait, and a still longer time for a girl to keep a secret. But Jo did both, and was just beginning to give up all hope of ever seeing her manuscript again, when a letter arrived which almost took her breath away, for on opening it, a check for one hundred dollars fell into her lap. For a minute she stared at it as if it had been a snake, then she read her letter and began to cry. Jo valued the kindly letter even more than the money, because after years of effort it was so pleasant to find that she had learned to do something well.

She electrified the family by appearing before them with the letter in one hand, the check in the other, announcing that she had won the prize. Of course there was a great jubilee, and when the story came everyone read and praised it. After her father had told her that the language was good and the tragedy quite thrilling, he shook his head, and said, "You can do better than this, Jo. Aim at the highest, and never mind the money."

"I think the money is the best part of it. What will you do with such a fortune?" asked Amy, regarding the magic slip of paper with a reverence.

"Send Beth and Mother to the seaside for a month or two," answered Jo promptly.

"Oh, how splendid! No, I can't, it would be so selfish," cried Beth, who had clapped her thin hands and taken a long breath, as if pining for fresh ocean breeze, then stopped herself and motioned away the check which her sister waved before her.

"Ah, but you shall go, I've set my heart on it. That's what I tried for, and that's why I succeeded. Besides, Marmee needs the change, and she won't leave you, so you must go. Won't it be fun to see you come home plump and rosy again? Hurrah for Dr. Jo, who always cures her patients!"

To the seaside they went, after much discussion, and though Beth didn't come home as plump and rosy as could be desired, she was much better, while Mrs. March declared she felt ten years younger. So Jo was satisfied with the investment of her prize money, and fell to work with a cheery spirit, bent on earning more of those delightful checks. She did earn several that year, and by the magic of a pen, her "rubbish" turned into comforts for them all. *The Duke's Daughter* paid the butcher's bill, *A Phantom Hand* put down a new carpet, and *The Curse of the Coventrys* proved the blessing of the Marches in the way of groceries and gowns.

Wealth is certainly a most desirable thing, but poverty has its sunny side, and neediness has inspired half the wise, beautiful, and useful blessings of the world. Jo ceased to envy richer girls. Encouraged by selling her little stories, she aimed at fame and fortune. She copied her novel for the fourth time and submitted it with fear and trembling to three publishers, and one of them said they would publish it on condition that she cut it down one-third and omit all the parts she particularly admired.

"Now I must either bundle it back into my tin box to mold, pay for printing it myself, or chop it up to suit purchasers and get what I can for it. Fame is a good thing, but cash is more convenient. What do you advise?" said Jo, calling a family council.

"Don't spoil your book, my girl, for there is more in it than you know, and the idea is well worked out. Let it wait and ripen," was her father's advice.

"It seems to me that Jo will profit more by experience than by waiting," said Mrs. March. "The praise and blame of outsiders will prove useful, even if she gets but little money."

"Yes," said Jo, knitting her brows, "that's just it. I've been fussing over the thing so long, I really don't know whether it's good, bad, or indifferent. It will be a great help to have cool, impartial persons take a look at it, and tell me what they think of it."

"I wouldn't leave out a word of it. You'll spoil it if you do, for it will be all a muddle if you don't explain as you go on," said Meg, who firmly believed that this book was the most remarkable novel ever written.

"But Mr. Allen says, 'Leave out the explanations, make it brief and dramatic, and let the characters tell the story,' "interrupted Jo, turning to the publisher's note.

"Do as he tells you, he knows what will sell, and we don't. Make a good, popular book, and get as much money as you can. By-and-by, when you've got a name, you can have philosophical people in your novels," said Amy, who took a strictly practical view of the subject.

"Well," said Jo, laughing, "if my people are philosophical, it isn't my fault, for I know nothing about such things. If I've got some of Father's wise ideas jumbled up with my romance, so much the better. Now, Beth, what do you say?"

"I should so like to see it printed soon" was all Beth said, and smiled in saying it. There was a wistful look in the eyes that never lost their childlike candor, which chilled Jo's heart for a minute with a foreboding fear, and that decided the matter.

So the young author laid her first-born on her table, and chopped it up as ruthlessly as any ogre. In the hope of pleasing everyone, she took everyone's advice. She cut out the description, the story links, and the fun. Then, to complete the ruin, she cut it down one-third, and sent the poor little book, like a picked robin, out into the big, busy world to seek its fate.

Well, it was printed, and she got three hundred dollars for it; likewise so much praise and blame that she was thrown into a state of bewilderment from which it took her some time to recover.

"You said, Mother, that criticism would help me. But I don't know whether I've written a promising book or broken all the ten commandments!" cried poor Jo, turning over a heap of reviews. "This man says, 'An exquisite book, full of truth, beauty, and earnestness; all is sweet, pure, and healthy,' and the next says, 'The theory of the book is bad, full of morbid fancies, occult ideas, and unnatural characters.' Now, as I had no theory of any kind, don't believe in the occult, and copied my characters from life, I don't see how he can be right. Another says, 'It's one of the best American novels which has appeared for years' (I know better than that) and the next asserts that 'though it is original, it is a dangerous book.' It isn't! Nearly all insist that I had a deep theory to expound, when I only wrote it for the pleasure and the money. I do hate to be so misjudged."

It was a hard time for sensitive, high-spirited Jo, who meant so well. But it did her good, for those whose opinion had real value gave her the criticism which is an author's best education. When the first soreness was over, she could laugh at her poor little book, yet believe in it still, and feel herself the wiser and stronger because of it.

"Not being a genius, like Keats, it won't kill me," she said stoutly, "and I've got the joke on my side, after all, for the parts that were taken straight out of real life are denounced as impossible, and the scenes that I made up out of my own silly head are pronounced true. So I'll comfort myself with that, and when I'm ready, I'll try again."

5

DOMESTIC EXPERIENCES

LIKE MOST OTHER YOUNG WIVES, Meg began her married life with the determination to be a model housekeeper. John should find home a paradise, always see a smiling face, dine elegantly every day, and never know the loss of a button. In spite of Meg's intentions, however, the paradise was not a tranquil one, because she fussed and bustled about so much that she was often too tired to smile. John got indigestion from too many elegant meals and demanded plain food. As for buttons, she soon learned to wonder where they went, shake her head over the carelessness of men, and threaten to make him sew them on himself.

They were happy, even after they discovered that they couldn't live on love alone. Then John concentrated on business, feeling the cares of the head of a family upon his shoulders, and Meg put on a big apron, and fell to work with more energy than discretion.

Sometimes her family was invited in to help eat up a too bounteous feast of successes, or Lotty would be privately sent away with a batch of failures, which were to be concealed from all eyes in the convenient stomachs of the little Hummels. An evening with John over the account books usually produced a temporary food lull during which the poor man was put through a course of bread pudding, hash, and warmed-over coffee, which tried his soul, although he bore it with praiseworthy fortitude.

Fired with a housewifely wish to have homemade preserves, she decided to make her own currant jelly. John was requested to order a dozen or so of little jars and an extra quantity of sugar, for their own currants were ripe and were to be attended to at once. As John firmly believed that "my wife" was equal to anything, home came four dozen delightful little jars, half a barrel of sugar, and a small boy to pick the currants. With her pretty hair tucked into a little cap, arms bared to the elbow, and a checked apron, the young housewife fell to work, feeling no doubts about her success. The array of jars amazed her at first, but Meg resolved to fill them all, and spent a long day boiling, straining, and fussing over her jelly. She did her best, she checked her recipe book, she racked her brain to remember what Hannah did that she left undone, she reboiled, resugared, and restrained, but that dreadful stuff wouldn't "jell."

She longed to run home and ask Mother to lend a hand, but John and she had agreed that they would never annoy anyone with their private problems or quarrels. They had laughed over that last word as if the idea was preposterous, but they followed the plan. So Meg wrestled alone with the impossible jelly all that hot summer day, and at five o'clock sat down in her topsy-turvy kitchen, wrung her sticky hands, lifted up her voice and wept.

Now, in the first flush of married life, Meg had often said, "Always feel free to bring a friend home. I shall always be prepared. There shall be no flurry, no scolding, no discomfort, but a neat house, a cheerful wife, and a good dinner. John, dear, never stop to ask me, invite whom you please." John glowed with pride to hear her say it, and felt what a blessed thing it was to have a superior wife. But, although they had had company from time to time, it never happened to be unexpected till now.

If John had not forgotten all about the jelly, it really would have been unpardonable for him to choose that day, of all the days in the year, to bring a friend home to dinner unexpectedly. Indulging in pleasant anticipation of his pretty wife running out to meet him, he escorted his friend to his mansion.

It is a world of disappointments, as John discovered when he reached the Dovecote. The front door usually stood hospitably open; now it was not only shut, but locked, and yesterday's mud still adorned the steps. The parlor windows were closed and curtained; no pretty wife sewing on the veranda, in white, with a distracting little bow in her hair, and no bright-eyed hostess, smiling a shy welcome as she greeted her guest. Nothing of the sort, for not a soul appeared but a boy asleep under the currant bushes.

"I'm afraid something has happened. Step into the garden, Scott, while I look for Mrs. Brooke," said John, alarmed at the silence and solitude.

Round the house he hurried, led by a pungent smell of burned sugar, and Mr. Scott strolled after him, with a strange look on his face. He paused discreetly at a distance when Brooke disappeared, but he could both see and hear, and being a bachelor, enjoyed the prospect mightily.

In the kitchen reigned confusion and despair. One edition of jelly was trickled from pot to pot, another lay upon the floor, and a third was burning gaily on the stove. Lotty was calmly eating bread with currant syrup, for the jelly was still in a hopelessly liquid state, while Mrs. Brooke, with her apron over her head, sat sobbing dismally.

"My dearest girl, what is the matter?" cried John, rushing in, with awful visions of scalded hands or bad news, and secret consternation at the thought of the guest in the garden.

"Oh, John, I am so tired and hot and cross and worried! I've been at it till I'm all worn out. Do come and help me or I shall die!" And the exhausted housewife cast herself upon his breast, giving him a sweet welcome in every sense of the word, for her apron had been baptized at the same time as the floor.

"Has anything dreadful happened?" asked the anxious John, tenderly kissing the little cap, which was all askew.

"Yes," sobbed Meg despairingly.

"Tell me quick, then. Don't cry, I can bear anything better than that. Out with it, love."

"The . . . the jelly won't jell and I don't know what to do!"

John Brooke laughed then as he never dared to laugh afterward, which put the finishing stroke to poor Meg's woe. "Is that all? Fling it out the window, and don't bother any more about it. I'll buy you quarts if you want it. For heaven's sake don't have hysterics, for I've brought Jack Scott home to dinner, and . . ."

John got no further, for Meg cast him off, and clasped her hands with a tragic gesture as she fell into a chair, exclaiming in a tone of mingled indignation, reproach, and dismay, "A man to dinner, and everything in a mess! John Brooke, how could you do such a thing?"

"Hush, he's in the garden! I forgot the confounded jelly, but it can't be helped now," said John.

"You ought to have sent word, or told me this morning, and you ought to have remembered how busy I was," continued Meg, for even turtledoves will peck when ruffled.

"I didn't know it this morning, and there was no time to send word, for I met him on the way out. You have always told me to do as I liked. I never tried it before, and hang me if I ever do again!" added John.

"I should hope not! Take him away at once. I can't see him and there isn't any dinner."

"Well, I like that! Where's the beef and vegetables I sent home, and the pudding you promised?" cried John, rushing to the larder.

"I hadn't time to cook anything. I meant to dine at Mother's. I'm sorry, but I was so busy." And Meg's tears began again.

John was a mild man, but he was human. After a long day's work to come home tired, hungry, and hopeful, to find a chaotic house, an empty table, and a cross wife was not exactly soothing. He restrained himself, however, and the little squall would have blown over, but for one unlucky word.

"If you will lend a hand, we'll pull through and have a good time yet. Don't cry, dear, but just fix us up something to eat. We're both as hungry as hunters, so we shan't mind what it is. Give us the cold meat, and bread and cheese—we won't ask for jelly."

He meant it for a good-natured joke, but the word *jelly* sealed his fate.

"It's like a man to propose cold meat and bread and cheese for company. I won't have anything of the sort in my house. Take that Scott up to Mother's, and tell him I'm away, sick, dead—anything. I won't see him, and you two can laugh at me and my jelly as much as you like." And having delivered her defiance all on one breath, Meg tossed down her apron and left for her room.

What those two creatures did in her absence, she never knew, but Mr. Scott was not taken "up to Mother's," and when Meg descended, after they had strolled away together, she found traces of a hasty snack. Lotty reported that they had eaten and laughed, and Mr. Brooke told her to throw away all the sweet stuff.

Meg longed to go and tell Mother, but loyalty to John, "who might be cruel, but nobody should know it," restrained her. She dressed herself prettily, and sat down to wait for John to come and be forgiven.

Unfortunately, John didn't see the matter in that light. He had carried it off as a good joke with Scott, but John was angry, though he did not show it. He felt that Meg had got him into a scrape, and then deserted him in his hour of need. "It wasn't fair to tell a man to bring folks home any time, with perfect freedom, and when he took you at your word, to flame up and blame him, and leave him in the lurch, to be laughed at or pitied." As he strolled home after seeing Scott off, a milder mood came over him. "Poor little thing! It was hard upon her when she tried so heartily to please me. She was wrong, of course, but then she was young. I must be patient and teach her." He hoped she had not gone home. For a minute he was ruffled again at the mere thought of it. Then the fear that Meg would cry herself sick softened his heart, and sent him on at a quicker pace, resolving to be calm and kind, but firm, and show her where she had failed in her duty.

Meg likewise resolved to be "calm and kind, but firm," and show him his duty. She longed to run to meet him, and beg pardon, and be kissed and comforted, as she was sure of being. But, of course, she did nothing of the sort, and when she saw John coming, began to hum quite naturally, as she rocked and sewed, like a lady of leisure in her best parlor.

John, feeling that his dignity demanded the first apology, came leisurely in and laid himself upon the sofa with the remark, "We are going to have a new moon, my dear."

"I've no objection."

A few other topics of general interest were introduced by Mr. Brooke and wet-blanketed by Mrs. Brooke, and conversation languished. John went to one window and sat down with his paper. Meg went to the other window, and sat down with her sewing. Neither spoke. Both looked "calm and firm," and both felt desperately uncomfortable.

"Oh dear," thought Meg, "married life is trying, and does need infinite patience as well as love, as Mother says." The word "Mother" reminded her of some of her mother's other advice.

"John is a good man, but he has his faults, and you must learn to see and bear with them, remembering your own. He has a temper, not like ours—one flash and then all over—but the white, still anger that is seldom stirred, but once kindled is hard to quench. Be careful, very careful, not to wake his anger against yourself, for peace and happiness depend on keeping his respect. Watch yourself, be the first to ask pardon if you both err, and guard against the little misunderstandings, and hasty words that often pave the way for bitter sorrow and regret."

These words came back to Meg as she sat sewing in the sunset. Thoughts of poor John coming home to such a scene melted her heart. She glanced at him with tears in her eyes, but he did not see them. She put down her work and got up, thinking, "I will be the first to say, 'Forgive me.' " She went slowly across the room, and stood by him, but he did not turn his head. For a minute she felt as if she really couldn't do it, then came the thought, "I'll do my part," and stooping down, she softly kissed her husband on the forehead. Of course that settled it. The penitent kiss was better than a world of words, and John had her on his knee in a minute, saying tenderly, "It was bad to laugh at the poor little jelly jars. Forgive me, dear, I never will again!"

But he did, oh bless you, yes, hundreds of times, and so did Meg, both declaring that it was the sweetest jelly they ever made, for family peace was preserved instead of currants.

After this, Meg had Mr. Scott to dinner by special invitation, on which occasion she was so gay and gracious, and made everything go off so charmingly, that Mr. Scott shook his head over the hardships of bachelorhood all the way home.

In the autumn, new trials and experiences came to Meg. Sallie Moffat renewed her friendship. It was pleasant, for in dull weather Meg often felt lonely. All were busy at home, John was absent till night, and she had nothing to do but sew, or read, or potter about. Sallie was kind, and often offered Meg pretty things, but Meg declined them, knowing that John wouldn't like it. Then this foolish little woman did what John disliked infinitely worse.

She knew her husband's income, and she loved to feel that he trusted her, not only with his happiness, but with what some men seem to value more—his money. But that autumn the serpent got into Meg's paradise, and tempted her like many a modern Eve, not with apples, but with clothes. Meg didn't like to be pitied and made to feel poor, and now and then she tried to console herself by buying something pretty, so that Sallie needn't think she had to economize. She always felt wicked after it, for the pretty things were seldom necessaries, but then they cost so little, it wasn't worth worrying about. At the end of the month, the sum total scared her.

John was busy that month and left the bills to her. The next month he was absent, but the third he had a grand quarterly settling up. A few days before, she had done a dreadful thing. Sallie had been buying silks, and here was a lovely, shimmering violet silk going at a bargain. Aunt March usually gave the sisters a present of twenty-five dollars apiece at New Year's and that was only a month to wait. Meg could borrow the other twenty-five from her household fund. She said "I'll take it," and it was cut off and paid for.

When she got home, the words "fifty dollars" seemed stamped like a pattern on the silk. She put it away, but it haunted her. When John got out his books that night, Meg's heart sank, and for the first time in her married life, she was afraid of her husband. John was undoing the old pocketbook which they called the "bank," when Meg, knowing that it was empty, stopped his hand, saying nervously, "You haven't seen my private expense book yet."

The little book was brought slowly out and laid down before him. Meg got behind his chair under pretense of smoothing the wrinkles out of his tired forehead, and standing there, she said, with her panic increasing with every word, "John, dear, I'm ashamed to show you my book, for I've really been dreadfully extravagant lately. Sallie advised my getting it, so I did, and my New Year's money will partly pay for it. But I was sorry after I'd done it, for I knew you'd think it wrong in me."

John laughed, and drew her round beside him, saying good-humoredly, "I'm proud of my wife's feet, and don't mind if she does pay eight or nine dollars for her boots, if they are good ones."

"It's worse than boots, it's a silk dress," she said, for she wanted the worst over.

She turned the page, pointing to the sum which would have been bad enough without the fifty, but which was appalling with that added. For a minute the room was still, then John said slowly, but she could feel it cost him an effort, "Well, I don't know that fifty is much for a dress, with all the trim you use to finish it off these days."

"It isn't made or trimmed," sighed Meg faintly, for a sudden recollection of the future costs overwhelmed her.

"Twenty-five yards of silk seems a good deal to cover one small woman," said John dryly.

"I know you are angry, John, but I can't help it. I don't mean to waste your money, and I didn't think things would count up so. I try to be contented, but it is hard, and I'm tired of being poor."

The last words were spoken so low she thought he did not hear them, but he did, and they wounded him deeply, for he had denied himself many pleasures for Meg's sake. She could have bitten her tongue out the minute she had said it, for John pushed the books away and got up, saying with a little quiver in his voice, "I was afraid of this. I do my best, Meg." If he had scolded her, or even shaken her, it would not have broken her heart like those few words. She ran to him and held him close, crying, with repentant tears, "Oh, John, I didn't mean it! It was so wicked, so untrue and ungrateful, how could I say it?"

He was kind, forgave her readily, and did not utter one reproach. But Meg knew that she had done and said a thing which would not be forgotten soon. John went on quietly afterward, just as if nothing had happened, except that he stayed in town later, and worked at night when she had gone to cry herself to sleep. A week of remorse nearly made Meg sick, and the discovery that John had canceled the order for his new overcoat reduced her to a state of despair. He had simply said, in answer to her surprised inquiries, "I can't afford it, my dear."

Meg said no more, but a few minutes after he found her in the hall with her face buried in the old coat, crying as if her heart would break.

Next day she put her pride in her pocket, went to Sallie, told the truth, and asked her to buy the silk as a favor. The good-natured Mrs.

Moffat willingly did so, and had the delicacy not to make her a present of it immediately afterward. Then Meg ordered the overcoat, and, when it arrived, she put it on and asked John how he liked her new silk gown. That overcoat was put on in the morning by a happy husband, and taken off at night by a most devoted little wife.

So the year rolled round, and at midsummer there came to Meg a new experience—the deepest and tenderest of a woman's life.

Laurie came sneaking into the kitchen of the Dovecote one Saturday, with an excited face, and was received with the clash of cymbals, for Hannah clapped her hands with a saucepan in one and the cover in the other.

"How's the little mamma? Where is everybody? Why didn't you tell me before I came home?" began Laurie in a loud whisper.

"Happy as a queen, the dear! Every soul of 'em is upstairs a worshipin'. Now you go into the parlor, I'll send 'em down to you."

Presently Jo appeared, proudly bearing a flannel bundle laid forth upon a large pillow. Jo's face was sober, but her eyes twinkled, and there was an odd sound in her voice.

"Shut your eyes and hold out your arms," she said invitingly.

Laurie backed into a corner, and put his hands behind him with an imploring gesture. "No, thank you, I'd rather not. I shall drop it or smash it, as sure as fate."

"Then you shan't see it," said Jo decidedly, turning as if to go.

"I will, I will! Only you must be responsible." Obeying orders, Laurie heroically shut his eyes while something was put into his arms. A peal of laughter from Jo, Amy, Mrs. March, Hannah, and John caused him to open them the next minute, to find himself holding two babies instead of one.

No wonder they laughed, for the expression on his face was funny enough to convulse a Quaker, as he stood and stared wildly with such dismay that Jo sat down on the floor and screamed.

"Twins!" was all he said for a minute, then turning to the women with an appealing look that was comically piteous, he added, "Take 'em quick, somebody! I'm going to laugh, and I shall drop 'em."

John rescued his babies, and marched up and down, with one on each arm, as if already initiated into the mysteries of baby-tending, while Laurie laughed till the tears ran down his cheeks.

"It's the best joke of the season, isn't it? I wouldn't have you told, for I set my heart on surprising you, and I flatter myself I've done it," said Jo, when she got her breath.

"I never was more staggered in my life. Isn't it fun? Are they boys? What are you going to name them? Let's have another look. Hold me up, Jo, for upon my life it's one too many for me," returned Laurie, regarding the infants with the air of a big, benevolent Newfoundland looking at a pair of kittens.

"Boy and girl. Aren't they beauties?" said the proud papa, beaming upon the little red squirmers as if they were featherless angels.

"Most remarkable children I ever saw. Which is which?" and Laurie bent to examine the prodigies.

"Amy put a blue ribbon on the boy and a pink on the girl, French fashion, so you can always tell. Besides, one has blue eyes and one brown. Kiss them, Uncle Teddy," said wicked Jo.

"I'm afraid they mightn't like it," began Laurie, with unusual timidity in such matters.

"Of course they will, they are used to it now. Do it this minute, sir!" commanded Jo, fearing he might propose a proxy.

Laurie screwed up his face and obeyed with a gingerly peck at each little cheek that produced another laugh and made the babies squeal.

"There, I knew they didn't like it! That's the boy, see him kick, he hits out with his fists like a good one. Now then, young Brooke, pitch into a man of your own size, will you!" cried Laurie, delighted with a poke in the face from a tiny fist, flapping aimlessly about.

"He's to be named John Laurence, and the girl Margaret, after mother and grandmother. We shall call her Daisy, so as not to have two Megs, and I suppose the boy will be Jack, unless we find a better name," said Amy, with aunt-like interest.

"Name him Demijohn, and call him 'Demi' for short," said Laurie.

"Daisy and Demi—just the thing! I knew Teddy would do it," cried Jo, clapping her hands.

Teddy certainly had done it that time, for the babies were Daisy and Demi from that day on.

6
CALLS

"I'VE DONE A GOOD MANY rash and foolish things in my life, but I don't think I ever was insane enough to say I'd make six calls in one day, when a single one upsets me for a week," Jo declared.

"Yes, you did, it was a bargain between us. I was to finish the crayon of Beth for you, and you were to go properly with me, and return our neighbors' visits."

Jo was absorbed in dressmaking, and she could use a needle as well as a pen. It was provoking to be ordered out to make calls in her best array on a warm July day. She hated calls of the formal sort, and never made any till Amy compelled her. In the present instance there was no escape; and having clashed her scissors rebelliously, while protesting that she smelled thunder and rain coming, she gave in and put away her work.

"Jo March, you are perverse enough to provoke a saint! You don't intend to make calls in that state, I hope," cried Amy, surveying her with amazement.

"Why not? I'm neat and cool and comfortable, quite proper for a dusty walk on a warm day. You can be as elegant as you please."

"Oh dear!" sighed Amy, "I'm sure it's no pleasure to me to go today, but it's a debt we owe society. I'll do anything for you, Jo, if you'll only dress yourself nicely, and come and help me. You can talk so well, look so aristocratic in your best things, and behave so beautifully, if you try, that I'm proud of you. I'm afraid to go alone. Do come and take care of me."

"You flatter and wheedle me. The idea of my being aristocratic and well-bred, and your being afraid to go anywhere alone! I don't know which is the most absurd. Well, I'll go if I must, and do my best."

"You're a perfect cherub! Now put on all your best things, and I'll tell you how to behave at each place. I want people to like you, and they would if you'd only try to be a little more agreeable. Do your hair the pretty way, and put the pink rose in your bonnet. Take your light gloves and the embroidered handkerchief."

Jo sighed as she rustled into her new organdy, frowned darkly at herself as she tied her bonnet strings in a bow, and wrestled viciously with pins as she put on her collar. When she had squeezed her hands into tight gloves with three buttons and a tassel, she turned to Amy with an imbecile expression and said, "I'm perfectly miserable, but if you consider me presentable, I die happy."

Jo revolved, and Amy gave a touch here and there, then fell back, with her head on one side, observing graciously, "Yes, you'll do. I'm so glad Aunt March gave you that lovely shawl. It's simple, but handsome, and those folds over the arm are really artistic. Is the point of my mantle in the middle, and have I looped my dress evenly? I like to show my boots, for my feet are pretty, though my nose isn't."

"You are a thing of beauty and a joy forever," said Jo, looking at the blue feather against the golden hair. "Am I to drag my best dress through the dust, or loop it up, please, ma'am?"

"Hold it up when you walk, but drop it in the house. The sweeping style suits you best, and you must learn to trail your skirts gracefully. You haven't half buttoned one cuff. You'll never look finished if you are not careful about the little details, for they make up the pleasing whole."

At last both were ready and sailed away, stopping at Meg's house to borrow a white parasol. "Now, Jo dear," Amy began, "the Chesters consider themselves elegant people, so I want you to put on your best deportment. Don't make any of your abrupt remarks, or do anything odd, will you? Just be calm, cool, and quiet."

"Let me see. 'Calm, cool, and quiet' . . . yes, I think I can promise that. I've played the part of a prim young lady on the stage."

Amy looked relieved, but naughtily Jo took her at her word, for during the first call she sat with every limb gracefully composed, every fold correctly draped, calm as a summer sea, cool as a snowbank, and as silent as a sphinx. In vain Mrs. Chester alluded to her "charming novel," and her daughters brought up parties, picnics, the opera, and the fashions. Each and all were answered by a smile, a bow, and a demure "Yes" or "No" with the chill on. In vain Amy telegraphed the word talk and administered secret pokes with her foot. Jo sat as if blandly unconscious of it all.

"What a haughty, uninteresting creature that oldest Miss March is!" one of the ladies remarked as the door closed upon their guests. Jo laughed noiselessly all through the hall.

"How could you mistake me so? I merely meant you to be properly dignified and composed, and you made yourself a perfect stone," complained Amy. "Try to be sociable at the Lambs', and be interested in whatever nonsense comes up. They move in the best society and are valuable persons for us to know."

"I'll gossip and giggle, and have horrors and raptures over any trifle you like. I rather enjoy this, and now I'll imitate what is called 'a charming girl.' See if the Lambs don't say, 'What a lively, nice creature that Jo March is!' "

When Jo turned freakish there was no knowing where she would stop. Amy felt anxious when she saw her sister skim into the next drawing room, kiss all the young ladies with effusion, beam graciously upon the young gentlemen, and join in the chat with a spirit which amazed her. Amy was taken possession of by Mrs. Lamb, who talked

Naughtily Jo took her at her word, for during the first call she sat . . .
as silent as a sphinx.

non-stop to her while a group gathered about Jo and broke into frequent peals of laughter. One may imagine Amy's suffering on overhearing fragments of this sort of conversation:

"She used to practice mounting, holding the reins, and sitting straight on an old saddle in a tree. Now she rides anything, for she doesn't know what fear is, and the stableman lets her have horses cheap because she trains them to carry ladies so well. She has such a passion for it, I often tell her if everything else fails she can be a horsebreaker, and get her living so."

Amy heard snatches of Jo's entertaining stories, but could not get away from Mrs. Lamb to stop her. After carrying on about Amy's rollicking and dangerous adventures with horses, Jo launched into Amy's other talents.

"There's nothing the child can't do. Why, she wanted a pair of blue boots for Sallie's party, so she just painted her soiled white ones the loveliest shade of sky blue you ever saw, and they looked exactly like satin."

"We read a story of yours the other day, and enjoyed it very much," observed the elder Miss Lamb, wishing to compliment Jo.

Any mention of her stories always had a bad effect upon Jo, who either grew rigid and looked offended, or changed the subject with a brusque remark, as now. "Sorry you could find nothing better to read. I write that rubbish because it sells, and ordinary people like it. Are you going to New York this winter?"

The minute Jo said this she saw her mistake, but fearing to make the matter worse, she suddenly interrupted three people by gushing, "Amy, we must go. Goodbye, dear, do come and see us. I don't dare to ask you, Mr. Lamb, but if you should come, I don't think I shall have the heart to send you away."

"Didn't I do that well?" asked Jo, with a satisfied air as they walked away.

"Nothing could have been worse" was Amy's crushing reply. "What possessed you to tell those stories about my saddle and all the rest of it?"

"Why, it's funny and amuses people. They know we are poor, so it's no use pretending that we have things as easy and fine as they do."

"You haven't a bit of proper pride, and never will learn when to hold your tongue and when to speak," said Amy despairingly.

Poor Jo looked abashed. "How shall I behave here?" she asked, as they approached the third mansion.

"Just as you please. I wash my hands of you," was Amy's short answer.

"Then I'll enjoy myself. The boys are at home," returned Jo gruffly.

Leaving Amy to entertain the hostess and Mr. Tudor, who happened to be calling likewise, Jo devoted herself to the young folks. She listened to college stories with deep interest, caressed pointers and poodles, and when one lad proposed a visit to his turtle tank, she went gladly.

Amy proceeded to enjoy herself to her heart's content. Mr. Tudor's uncle had married an English lady who was third cousin to a living lord, and Amy regarded the whole family with great respect. But even the satisfaction of talking with a distant connection of the British nobility did not render Amy forgetful of time, and when the proper number of minutes had passed, she reluctantly tore herself from this aristocratic society, and looked about for Jo, fervently hoping that her incorrigible sister would not be found in any position which should bring disgrace upon the name of March.

It might have been worse, but Amy considered it bad, for Jo sat on the grass, with an encampment of boys about her, and a dirty-footed dog reposing on her skirt, as she related one of Laurie's pranks to her admiring audience. One small child was poking turtles with Amy's cherished parasol, a second was eating gingerbread over Jo's best bonnet, and a third playing ball with her gloves. But all were enjoying themselves.

"Why do you always avoid Mr. Tudor?" asked Amy as they were leaving. "You gave him a cool nod, and just now you bowed and smiled in the politest way to Tommy Chamberlain, whose father keeps a grocery store. If you had just reversed the nod and the bow, it would have been right."

"I neither like, respect, nor admire Tudor, though his grandfather's uncle's nephew's niece was third cousin to a lord. He puts on airs, snubs his sisters, worries his father, and doesn't speak respectfully of his mother. Tommy is poor and bashful and good and clever. I think well of him, and like to show that I do, for he is a gentleman in spite of the brown-paper parcels he delivers."

Jo was relieved that the next two families were absent, and they left their family calling cards that they carried for that purpose.

"Now let us go home, and never mind Aunt March today. We can run down there any time, and it's really a pity to trail through the dust in our best bibs and tuckers, when we are tired and cross."

"Speak for yourself, if you please. Aunt likes to have us pay her the compliment of coming in style, and making a formal call. It's a little thing to do, but it gives her pleasure, and I don't believe it will hurt your things half so much as letting dirty dogs and clumping boys spoil them. Stoop down, and let me take the crumbs off your bonnet."

"What a good girl you are, Amy!" said Jo, with a glance from her own damaged costume to that of her sister, which was fresh and spotless still. "I wish it was as easy for me to do little things to please people as it is for you. I wait for a chance to do a big favor and skip the small ones; but they do the most good, I fancy."

Amy smiled and was mollified at once, saying, "Women should learn to be agreeable, particularly poor ones, for they have no other way of repaying the kindnesses they receive. If you'd practice that you'd be better liked than I am, because there is more of you."

"It's easier for me to risk my life for a person than to be pleasant to him when I don't feel like it. It's a great misfortune to have such strong likes and dislikes, isn't it?"

56

"I don't mind saying that I don't approve of Tudor any more than you do, but there is no use in making yourself disagreeable because he is. If we were women of wealth and position, it might be different."

"So we are to smile at things and people we detest, merely because we are not millionaires, are we? That's a nice sort of morality."

"I can't argue about it. I only know that it's the way of the world, and people who set themselves against it only get laughed at for their pains. I don't like reformers, and I hope you will never try to be one."

"I do like them, and I shall be one if I can, for the world would never get on without them. You will get on the best, but I shall have the liveliest time of it."

"Well, compose yourself now, and don't worry Aunt with your new ideas."

"I'll try not to, but I'm always possessed to burst out with some particularly blunt speech before her. It's my doom, and I can't help it."

They found Aunt Mary Carrol with the old lady; their look betrayed that they had been talking about their nieces. Jo was not in a good humor, but Amy was in a most angelic frame of mind. This amiable spirit was felt at once, and both the aunts "my deared" her affectionately, thinking, "That child improves every day."

"Are you going to help with the charity fair, dear?" asked Mrs. Carrol, as Amy sat down beside her with the confiding air elderly people like so well in the young.

"Yes, Aunt. Mrs. Chester asked me if I would, and I offered to tend a table, as I have nothing but my time to give."

"I'm not," put in Jo decidedly. "The Chesters think it's a great favor to allow us to help with their high society fair. I wonder you consented, Amy, they only want you to work."

"I am willing to work. It's for the freed slaves as well as the Chesters, and I think it very kind of them to let me share the labor and the fun. Accepting favors does not trouble me when the favors are well meant."

"Quite right and proper. I like your grateful spirit, my dear. It's a pleasure to help people who appreciate our efforts. Some do not, and that is discouraging," observed Aunt March, looking over her spectacles at Jo, who sat apart, rocking herself, with a somewhat morose expression.

If Jo had only known what a great happiness was wavering in the balance, she would have turned dovelike in a minute. But, unfortunately, we cannot see what goes on in the minds of our friends. Better for us that we cannot as a general thing, but now and then it would be such a comfort, such a saving of time and temper. By her next words, Jo deprived herself of several years of pleasure.

"I don't like favors, they oppress and make me feel like a slave. I'd rather do everything for myself and be perfectly independent."

"Ahem!" coughed Aunt Carrol softly, with a look at Aunt March.

"I told you so," said Aunt March, with a decided nod to Aunt Carrol.

Mercifully unconscious of what she had done, Jo sat with her nose in the air, a rebellious pose which was anything but inviting.

"Do you speak French, dear?" asked Mrs. Carrol, laying her hand on Amy's.

"Pretty well, thanks to Aunt March, who lets Esther talk to me as often as I like," replied Amy, with a grateful look at the old lady.

"How are you with languages?" asked Mrs. Carrol of Jo.

"Don't know a word. I'm stupid about studying anything, can't bear French, it's such a slippery, silly sort of language," was the brusque reply.

Another look passed between the ladies, and Aunt March said to Amy, "You are strong and well, now, dear, I believe? Eyes don't trouble you any more, do they?"

"Not at all, thank you, ma'am. I'm very well, and mean to do great things next winter, so that I may be ready for Rome, whenever that joyful time arrives."

"Good girl! You deserve to go, and I'm sure you will some day," said Aunt March, with an approving pat on the head, as Amy picked up her ball of yarn for her.

"Crosspatch, draw the latch. Sit by the fire and spin," squalled Polly, bending down from his perch on the back of her chair to peep into Jo's face, with such a comical air of impertinent inquiry that it was impossible to keep from laughing.

"Most observing bird," said the old lady.

"Come and take a walk, my dear!" cried Polly, hopping toward the china closet, where there was some lump sugar.

"Thank you, I will. Come, Amy." And Jo brought the visit to an end, feeling more strongly than ever that calls did have a bad effect upon her. She shook hands in a gentlemanly manner, but Amy kissed both the aunts, and the girls departed, leaving behind them the impression of shadow and sunshine.

That impression caused Aunt March to say, as they vanished, "You'd better do it, Mary. I'll supply the money," and Aunt Carrol to reply decidedly, "I certainly will, if her father and mother consent."

7
CONSEQUENCES

MRS. CHESTER'S FAIR WAS SO ELEGANT and exclusive that it was a great honor to be asked to be in charge of a table. Amy was asked, but Jo was not, which was fortunate for everyone.

Everything went on smoothly till the day before the fair opened, then there occurred one of the little skirmishes which it is almost impossible to avoid, when some twenty-five women, old and young, with all their private stresses and strains, try to work together.

May Chester was jealous of Amy because the latter was a greater favorite than herself. Then Amy's dainty pen-and-ink work entirely eclipsed May's painted vases—that was one thorn. Then Mr. Tudor had danced four times with Amy at a late party and only once with May—that was thorn number two. But what rankled most was a rumor that the March girls had made fun of her at the Lambs'. All the blame of this should have fallen upon Jo, for her gushy goodbye had sounded like May Chester, and the Lambs had noticed.

Amy's dismay can be imagined when the evening before the fair, as she was putting the last touches to the art table, Mrs. Chester, who resented the supposed ridicule of her daughter, said in a bland tone but with a cold look, "I find, dear, that there is some feeling among the young ladies that as this is the most prominent table of all, my daughters should take it. I'm sorry, but I know you are too sincerely interested in the cause to mind a little personal disappointment, and you shall have another table if you like."

Mrs. Chester had fancied beforehand that it would be easy to deliver this little speech, but when the time came, she found it difficult to utter it naturally, with Amy's unsuspicious eyes looking straight at her, full of surprise and trouble.

Amy said quietly, feeling hurt, and showing that she did, "Perhaps you had rather I took no table at all?"

"Now, my dear, don't have any ill feeling, I beg. I feel very grateful for your efforts to make the art table so pretty and I will see that you have a good place elsewhere. Wouldn't you like the flower table? The little girls who undertook it are discouraged. The flower table is always attractive, you know."

"Especially to gentlemen," added May, with a look which enlightened Amy as to one cause of her sudden fall from favor. She colored angrily, but answered with unexpected amiability, "As you please, Mrs. Chester. I'll give up my place here at once, and attend to the flowers, if you like."

"You can put your own things on your own table, if you prefer," began May, feeling a little conscience-stricken as she looked at the pretty rocks, painted shells, and quaint illuminations Amy had so carefully made and so gracefully arranged. Amy mistook her meaning and said quickly, "Oh, certainly, if they are in your way." Sweeping her contributions into her apron, pell-mell, she walked off, feeling insulted past forgiveness.

"Now she's mad. Oh, dear, I wish I hadn't asked you to speak, Mamma," said May, looking at the empty spaces on her table.

"Girls' quarrels are soon over," returned her mother, feeling a trifle ashamed of her own part in this one, as well she might.

The little girls hailed Amy and her treasures with delight. But everything seemed against her. It was late, and she was tired, and the little girls were only hindrances, making a great deal of confusion in their efforts to help. The evergreen arch wouldn't stay firm after she got it up, but wiggled and threatened to tumble down on her head when the hanging baskets were filled. Her best tile got a splash of water, which left a brown tear on the Cupid's cheek. She bruised her hands with hammering, and got cold working in a draft. Any girl reader who has suffered similar troubles will sympathize with poor Amy.

There was great indignation at home when she told her story that evening. Her mother said it was a shame, but told her she had done right, Beth declared she wouldn't go to the fair at all, and Jo demanded why she didn't take all her pretty things and leave those mean people to get on without her.

"Because they are mean is no reason why I should be. I hate such things, and though I think I've a right to be hurt, I don't intend to show it. That will work better than angry speeches or huffy actions, won't it, Marmee?"

In spite of various temptations, Amy adhered to her resolution all the next day, bent on conquering her enemy by kindness. She began well. As she arranged her table that morning, she took up her pet production—a little book, with an antique cover her father had found among his treasures, and in which on leaves of vellum she had beautifully illuminated different sayings. As she turned the pages, her eye fell upon one verse that made her stop and think. Framed in a brilliant scrollwork of scarlet, blue, and gold, with little spirits of good will helping one another up and down among the thorns and flowers, were the words, "Thou shalt love thy neighbor as thyself."

"I ought, but I don't," thought Amy, as her eye went from the bright page to May's discontented face behind the big vases. Amy stood a minute, turning the pages in her hand, reading good and helpful words which are never out of season. Her conscience preached her a little sermon from that text, then and there, and she did what many of us do not always do—took the sermon to heart, and straightway put it in practice.

A group of girls were standing about May's table, admiring the pretty things, and Amy knew they were speaking of her, hearing one side of the story and judging her. Then she heard May say sorrowfully, "It's too bad, for there is no time to make other things, and I don't want to fill up with odds and ends. The table was complete then—now it's spoiled."

"I dare say she'd put them back if you asked her," suggested someone.

"How could I after all the fuss?" began May, but she did not finish, for Amy's voice came across the hall, saying pleasantly, "You may have them, and welcome, if you want them. They belong to your table rather than mine. Here they are, please take them, and forgive me if I was hasty in carrying them away last night."

As she spoke, Amy returned her contribution, with a nod and a smile, and hurried away again.

"Now, I call that lovely of her, don't you?" cried one girl.

May's answer was inaudible, but another young lady, whose temper was evidently a little soured by making lemonade, added, with a disagreeable laugh, "Very lovely, for she knew she wouldn't sell them at her own table."

It was a long day and a hard one to Amy, as she sat behind her table, often alone, for the little girls deserted very soon. Few cared to buy flowers in summer, and her bouquets began to droop long before night.

The art table was the most attractive in the room. There was a crowd about it all day long, and the workers were constantly flying to and fro with important faces and rattling money boxes. Amy often looked wistfully across, longing to be there where she felt at home and happy, instead of in a corner with nothing to do.

When she went home for supper, her mother gave her an extra cordial cup of tea, Beth helped her dress up and made a charming little wreath for her hair, while Jo astonished the family by dressing up and hinting darkly that the tables were about to be turned.

"Don't do anything rude, pray, Jo. Let it all pass and behave yourself," begged Amy, as she departed early.

"I merely intend to make myself entrancingly agreeable to everyone I know, and to keep them in your corner as long as possible. Teddy and his boys will lend a hand, and we'll have a good time yet," returned Jo, leaning over the gate to watch for Laurie. Presently familiar tramping was heard in the dusk, and she ran out to meet him.

"Is that my boy?"

"As sure as this is my girl!" And Laurie tucked her hand under his arm with the air of a man whose every wish was gratified.

"Oh, Teddy, such doings!" And Jo told Amy's wrongs with sisterly zeal.

"A flock of our fellows are going to drive over by-and-by, and I'll be hanged if I don't make them buy every flower she's got, and camp down before her table afterward," said Laurie, with warmth.

"The flowers are not at all nice, Amy says, and the fresh ones may not arrive in time," observed Jo in a disgusted tone.

"Didn't Hayes give you the best out of our gardens? I told him to."

"I didn't know that. He forgot, I suppose, and, as your grandpa was poorly, I didn't like to worry him by asking, though I did want some."

"Now, Jo, how could you think there was any need of asking? They are just as much yours as mine. Don't we always go halves in everything?" began Laurie, in the tone that always made Jo turn prickly.

"Gracious, I hope not! Half of some of your things wouldn't suit me at all. But we mustn't stand philandering here. I've got to help Amy, so you go and make yourself splendid, and if you'll be so kind as to let Hayes take a few nice flowers up to the Hall, I'll bless you forever."

"Couldn't you do it now?" asked Laurie, so suggestively that Jo shut the gate in his face with inhospitable haste, and called through the bars, "Go away, Teddy. I'm busy."

Hayes sent up a wilderness of flowers, with a lovely basket arranged in his best manner for a centerpiece. Then the March family turned out en masse, and people not only came, but stayed, laughing at Jo's nonsense, admiring Amy's taste, and apparently enjoying themselves. Laurie and his friends gallantly made that corner the liveliest spot in the room. Amy was in her element now, and was as sprightly and gracious as possible—coming to the conclusion, about that time, that virtue was its own reward, after all.

Jo circulated about the hall, picking up various bits of gossip, which enlightened her about the change of tables. She reproached herself for her share of the ill feeling and resolved to clear Amy as soon as possible. She also discovered what Amy had done about the things in the morning. As she passed the art table, she glanced over it for her sister's things, but saw no signs of them.

"Tucked away out of sight, I dare say," thought Jo, who could forgive her own hurts, but hotly resented any insult offered to her family.

"Good evening, Miss Jo. How does Amy get on?" asked May, for she wanted to show that she also could be generous.

"She has sold everything she had that was worth selling, and now she is enjoying herself. The flower table is always attractive, you know, especially to gentlemen."

Jo couldn't resist giving that little slap, but May took it so meekly she regretted it a minute after, and fell to praising May's big vases, which still remained unsold.

"Is Amy's illumination anywhere about? I took a fancy to buy that for Father," said Jo, anxious to learn the fate of her sister's work.

"Everything of Amy's sold long ago. I took care that the right people saw them, and they made a nice little sum of money for us," returned May, who had overcome temptations, as well as Amy, that day.

Much gratified, Jo rushed back to tell the good news, and Amy looked both touched and surprised by the report of May's words and manner.

"Now, gentlemen, I want you to go and do your duty by the other tables as generously as you have by mine—especially the art table," she said.

"To hear is to obey, but March is fairer far than May," said Parker, making a frantic effort to be both witty and tender.

"Buy the vases," whispered Amy to Laurie, as a final heaping of coals of fire on her enemy's head.

To May's great delight, Mr. Laurence not only bought the vases, but roamed throughout the hall with one under each arm. The other gentlemen wandered helplessly about afterward, burdened with wax flowers, painted fans, and other useful purchases.

The fair was pronounced a success, and when May bade Amy good night, she did not gush as usual, but gave her an affectionate kiss, and a look which said, "Forgive and forget." That satisfied Amy, and when she got home she found the vases paraded on the parlor mantel with a great bouquet in each. "The reward of merit for a magnanimous March," as Laurie announced with a flourish.

"You've a deal more principle and generosity and nobleness of character than I ever gave you credit for, Amy. You've behaved sweetly, and I respect you with all my heart," said Jo warmly, as they brushed their hair together late that night.

"Yes, we all do, and love her for being so ready to forgive. It must have been dreadfully hard, after working so long and setting your heart on selling your own pretty things. I don't believe I could have done it as kindly as you did," added Beth from her pillow.

"Why, girls, I only did as I'd be done by. You laugh at me when I say I want to be a lady, but I mean a true gentlewoman in mind and manners, and I try to do it as far as I know how. I can't explain exactly, but I want to be above little meannesses and faults. I'm far from it now, but I do my best, and hope in time to be what Mother is."

Amy spoke earnestly, and Jo said, with a cordial hug, "I understand now what you mean, and I'll never laugh at you again. I'll take lessons of you in true politeness, for you've learned the secret, I believe. You'll get your reward some day, and no one will be more delighted than I shall."

A week later Amy did get her reward, and poor Jo found it hard to be delighted. A letter came from Aunt Carrol, and Mrs. March's face was shining so that Jo and Beth demanded what the glad tidings were.

"Aunt Carrol is going abroad next month, and wants . . ."

"Me to go with her!" burst in Jo, flying out of her chair in an uncontrollable rapture.

"No, dear, not you. It's Amy."

"Oh, Mother! She's too young, it's my turn first. I've wanted it so long. It would do me so much good, and be so altogether splendid. I must go."

"I'm afraid it's impossible, Jo. Aunt says Amy, decidedly."

"It's always so. Amy has all the fun and I have all the work. It isn't fair, oh, it isn't fair!" cried Jo passionately.

"I'm afraid it is partly your own fault, dear. Aunt Carrol writes, as if quoting something you had said: 'I planned at first to ask Jo, but as "favors burden her" and she "hates French" I think I won't venture to invite her. Amy is more docile, will make a good companion for Flo, and receive gratefully any help the trip may give her.' "

"Oh, my tongue, my abominable tongue! Why can't I learn to keep it quiet?" groaned Jo, remembering words which had been her undoing.

When she had heard the explanation of the quoted phrases, Mrs. March said sorrowfully, "I wish you could have gone, but there is no hope of it this time, so don't sadden Amy's pleasure."

"I'll try," said Jo, blinking hard as she knelt down to pick up the basket she had joyfully upset. "I'll try not only to seem glad, but to be so, and not grudge her one minute of happiness. But it won't be easy." And poor Jo wet the little fat pincushion she held with several bitter tears.

"Jo, dear, I'm very selfish, but I'm glad you are not going quite yet," whispered Beth, embracing her, basket and all, with a clinging touch and loving face. Jo felt comforted in spite of the sharp regret that made her want to box her own ears, and humbly beg Aunt Carrol to burden her with this favor, and see how gratefully she would bear it.

By the time Amy came in, Jo was able to take her part in the family jubilation—not as heartily as usual, perhaps. The young lady herself went about in a solemn sort of rapture, and began to sort her colors and pack her pencils that evening, leaving such trifles as clothes, money, and passports to those less absorbed in visions of art.

"It isn't a mere pleasure trip to me, girls," she said impressively, as she scraped her best palette. "It will decide my career, for if I have any genius, I shall find it out in Rome, and will do something to prove it."

"Suppose you haven't?" said Jo, sewing away, with red eyes, at the new collars which were to be handed over to Amy.

"Then I shall come home and teach drawing for my living."

"No, you won't. You hate hard work, and you'll marry some rich man and come home to sit in the lap of luxury all your days," said Jo.

"I'm sure I wish your prediction would come true, for if I can't be an artist myself, I should like to be able to help those who are," said Amy, as if the part of Lady Bountiful would suit her better than that of a poor drawing teacher. "Would you like to go?"

"Rather!"

"Well, in a year or two I'll send for you, and we'll dig in the Forum for relics, and carry out all the plans we've made so many times."

"Thank you, I'll remind you of your promise when that joyful day comes, if it ever does," returned Jo, accepting the vague offer as gratefully as she could.

There was not much time for preparation, and the house was in a ferment till Amy was off. Jo bore up well till the last flutter of blue ribbon vanished, when she retired to her refuge, the garret, and cried till she couldn't cry any more. Amy likewise bore up stoutly till the steamer sailed. Then, just as the gangway was about to be withdrawn, it suddenly came over her that a whole ocean was soon to roll between her and those who loved her best, and she clung to Laurie, the last lingerer, saying with a sob, "Oh, take care of them for me, and if anything should happen . . ."

"I will, and if anything happens, I'll come and comfort you," whispered Laurie, little dreaming that he would be called upon to keep his word.

So Amy sailed away to find the Old World, which is always new and beautiful to young eyes, while her father and friend watched her from the shore, fervently hoping that none but gentle fortunes would befall the happy-hearted girl, who waved her hand to them till they could see nothing but the summer sunshine dazzling on the sea.

8

OUR FOREIGN CORRESPONDENT

LONDON

Dearest people,

Here I really sit at a front window of the Bath Hotel, Piccadilly, London.

Crossing the Atlantic Ocean was all heavenly, but I was glad to see the Irish coast, and found it lovely, so green and sunny. It was early in the morning, but I didn't regret getting up to see it, for the bay was full of little boats, the shore so picturesque, and a rosy sky overhead. I never shall forget it. After that we landed in England.

We only stopped at Liverpool a few hours. It's a dirty, noisy place, and I was glad to leave it. The train trip was like riding through a long picture gallery, full of lovely landscapes. The farmhouses were my delight, with thatched roofs, ivy up to the eaves, latticed windows, and stout women with rosy children at the doors. The cattle looked more tranquil than ours, as they stood knee-deep in clover, and the hens had a contented cluck, as if they never got nervous. Such perfect color I never saw—the grass so green, sky so blue, grain so yellow, woods so dark—I was in a rapture all the way. So was Flo, and we kept bouncing from one side to the other, trying to see everything while we were whisking along at the rate of sixty miles an hour. Aunt was tired and went to sleep, but Uncle read his guidebook, and wouldn't be astonished at anything. This is the way we went on: Amy, flying up, "Oh, that must be Kenilworth Castle, that gray place among the trees!" Flo, darting to my window, "How sweet! We must go there some time, won't we, Papa!" Uncle, calmly admiring his boots, "No, my dear, not unless you want beer. That's a brewery."

A pause, then Flo cried out, "Bless me, there's a gallows and a man going up." "Where, where?" shrieks Amy, staring out at two tall posts with a crossbeam and some dangling chains. "Coal mine equipment," remarks Uncle, with a twinkle of the eye. "Here's a lovely flock of lambs all lying down," says Amy. "See, Papa, aren't they pretty!" added Flo sentimentally. "Geese, young ladies," returns Uncle.

Of course it rained when we got to London, and there was nothing to be seen but fog and umbrellas. We rested, unpacked, and shopped a little between the showers. Aunt Mary got me some new things, for I came off in such a hurry I wasn't half ready. A white hat and blue feather, a muslin dress to match, and the loveliest mantle you ever saw. Shopping in Regent Street is perfectly splendid. Things seem so cheap—nice ribbons only six pence a yard. I laid in a stock, but shall get my gloves in Paris. Doesn't that sound sort of elegant and rich?

Flo and I, for the fun of it, ordered a hansom cab, while Aunt and Uncle were out, and went for a drive, though we learned afterward that it wasn't the thing for young ladies to ride in them alone. The man drove so fast that Flo was frightened, and told me to stop him. But he was up outside behind somewhere, and I couldn't get at him. He didn't hear me call, nor see me flap my parasol in front, and there we were, helpless, rattling away, and whirling around corners at a breakneck pace. At last, in my despair, I saw a little door in the roof, and on poking it open, a red eye appeared, and a beery voice said, "Now then, mum?"

I gave my order as soberly as I could, and slamming down the door, with an "Aye, aye, mum," the man made his horse walk, as if going to a funeral. I poked again and said, "A little faster," then off he went, helter-skelter as before, and we resigned ourselves to our fate.

Today was clear, and we went to Hyde Park. The Duke of Devonshire lives near, and the Duke of Wellington's house is not far off. Such sights as I saw! In the afternoon to Westminster Abbey, but don't expect me to describe it, that's impossible—so I'll only say it was sublime! This evening we are going to the theater, which will be an appropriate end to the happiest day of my life.

Midnight

It's late, but I can't let my letter go in the morning without telling you what happened. Who do you think came at tea time? Laurie's English friends, Fred and Frank Vaughn! I was so surprised, for I wouldn't have known them but for the cards. Both are tall fellows with whiskers, Fred handsome in the English style, and Frank much better, for he only limps slightly, and uses no crutches. They had heard from Laurie where we were to be. They went to the theater with us, and we did have such a good time, for Frank devoted himself to Flo, and Fred and I talked over past, present, and future fun as if we had known each other all our days. Tell Beth Frank asked about her, and was sorry to hear of her ill health. Fred laughed when I spoke of Jo, and sent his "respectful compliments." Neither of them had forgotten Camp Laurence, or the fun we had there. What ages ago it seems, doesn't it?

Aunt is tapping on the wall for the third time, so I must stop. I really feel like a dissipated London fine lady, writing here so late, with my room full of pretty things, and my head a jumble of parks, theaters, new gowns, and gallant creatures who say "Ah!" and twirl their blond mustaches with the true English lordliness. I long to see you all, and in spite of my nonsense am, as ever, your loving

Amy

Paris

Dear Girls,

In my last letter I told you about our London visit—how kind the Vaughns were, and what pleasant parties they made for us. I enjoyed the trips to Hampton Court and the Kensington Museum more than anything else, for I saw rooms full of pictures by Raphael, Turner, Lawrence, Reynolds, Hogarth, and the other great artists. The day in Richmond Park was charming, for we had a regular English picnic, and I had more splendid oaks and groups of deer than I could sketch. I also heard a nightingale and saw larks. We "did" London to our hearts' content, thanks to Fred and Frank. The Vaughns hope to meet us in Rome next winter, and I shall be dreadfully disappointed if they don't, for Grace and I are great friends, and the boys very nice fellows—especially Fred.

Well, we were hardly settled here, when he turned up again, saying he had come for a holiday, and was going to Switzerland. We are glad he came, for he speaks French like a native, and I don't know what we should do without him. Uncle doesn't know ten words, and insists on talking English very loud, as if that would make people understand him. Aunt's pronunciation is old-fashioned, and Flo and I, though we flattered ourselves that we knew a good deal, find we don't, and are grateful to have Fred do the "parley vooing," as Uncle calls it.

Such delightful times as we are having! Sight-seeing from morning till night, stopping for nice lunches in the cafes, and meeting with all sorts of droll adventures. Rainy days I spend in the Louvre, reveling in pictures. I've seen Napoleon's cocked hat and gray coat, his baby's cradle, and his old toothbrush. Also I've seen Marie Antoinette's little shoe, Charlemagne's sword, and many other interesting things. I'll talk for hours about them when I come, but haven't time to write.

I've seen the imperial family several times—the emperor an ugly, hard-looking man. the empress pale and pretty, but dressed in bad taste, I thought—purple dress, green hat, and yellow gloves.

We often walk in the Tuileries Gardens, for they are lovely, though the antique Luxembourg Gardens suit me better. Our rooms are on the Rue de Rivoli, and sitting on the balcony, we look up and down the long, brilliant street. It is so pleasant that we spend our evenings talking there when too tired with our day's work to go out. Fred is entertaining, and is altogether the most agreeable young man I ever knew—except Laurie, whose manners are more charming. I wish Fred was dark, for I don't fancy light men. However, the Vaughns are rich and come of an excellent family, so I won't find fault with their yellow hair, as my own is yellower.

Next week we are off to Germany and Switzerland, and as we shall travel fast, I shall only be able to give you hasty letters. Adieu, I embrace you tenderly.

Votre Amie

Heidelberg

My dear Mamma,

Having a quiet hour before we leave for Berne, I'll try to tell you what has happened, for some of it is very important, as you will see.

The sail up the Rhine was perfect, and I haven't words beautiful enough to describe it. At Coblenz we had a lovely time, for some students from Bonn, with whom Fred got acquainted on the boat, gave us a serenade. It was a moonlight night, and about one o'clock Flo and I were waked by the most delicious music under our windows. We flew up, and hid behind the curtains, but sly peeps showed us Fred and the students singing away down below. It was the most romantic thing I ever saw—the river, the bridge of boats, the great fortress opposite, moonlight everywhere, and music fit to melt a heart of stone.

When they were done we threw down some flowers, and saw them scramble for them, kiss their hands to the invisible ladies, and go laughing away. Next morning Fred showed me one of the crumpled flowers in his vest pocket, and looked very sentimental. I laughed at him, and said I didn't throw it, but Flo, so he tossed it out of the window. I'm afraid I'm going to have trouble with that boy.

Fred lost some money gambling at Baden-Baden, and I scolded him. He needs someone to look after him when Frank is not with him. Kate said once she hoped he'd marry soon, and I agree. Frankfurt was delightful. I saw Goethe's house and Schiller's statue, but I would have enjoyed them more if I had known about them. I ought to have read more, for I find I don't know anything, and it mortifies me.

Now comes the serious part—for it happened here, and Fred is just gone. He has been so kind and jolly that we all got quite fond of him. I've begun to feel that the moonlight walks, balcony talks, and daily adventures were something more to him than fun. I haven't flirted, Mother, truly. I can't help it if people like me. Now I know the girls say, "Oh, the mercenary little wretch!" but I've made up my mind, and, if Fred asks me, I shall accept him, though I'm not madly in love. I like him, and we get on comfortably together. He is handsome, young, clever enough, and rich—ever so much richer than the Laurences. His family are all kind, well-bred, generous people, and they like me. Fred, as the eldest twin, will have the estate, I suppose, and such a splendid one as it is! A city house in a fashionable street, not so showy as our big houses, but twice as comfortable and full of solid luxury, such as English people believe in. I've seen the silver service, the family jewels, the old servants, and pictures of the country place, with its park, great house, lovely grounds, and fine horses. Oh, it would be all I should ask! I may be mercenary, but I hate poverty, and don't mean to bear it a minute longer than I can help. One of us must marry well. Meg didn't, Jo won't, Beth can't yet, so I shall, and make everything cozy all round. I wouldn't marry a man I hated or despised—you may be sure of that. And though Fred is not my model hero, he does very well, and in time I should get fond enough of him if he was fond of me, and let me do just as I liked.

Well, last evening we went up to the castle about sunset—at least all of us but Fred, who was to meet us there after going to the post office for letters. We had a charming time poking about the ruins and the beautiful gardens made by the elector long ago for his English wife. I liked the great terrace best, for the view was divine, so while the rest went to see the rooms inside, I sat there trying to sketch the gray stone lion's head on the wall, with scarlet woodbine sprays hanging round it. I felt as if I'd got into a romance, sitting there, watching the Neckar River rolling through the valley, listening to the music of the Austrian band below, and waiting for my lover, like a real storybook girl. I had a feeling that something was going to happen and I was ready for it. I didn't feel blushy or quakey, but quite cool and only a little excited.

By-and-by I heard Fred's voice, and then he came hurrying through the great arch to find me. He said he'd just got a letter begging him to come home, for Frank was very ill, so he was going at once on the night train and only had time to say goodbye. I was disappointed, but only for a minute because he said, as he shook hands—and said it in a way that I could not mistake—"I shall soon come back. You won't forget me, Amy?"

I didn't promise, but I looked at him, and he seemed satisfied, and there was no time for anything but goodbyes, for he was off in an hour, and we all miss him very much. I think, from something he once hinted, that he had promised his father not to propose yet a while, for he is a rash boy, and the old gentleman dreads a foreign daughter-in-law. We shall soon meet in Rome, and then, if I don't change my mind, I'll say, "Yes, thank you" when he says, "Will you, please?"

Of course this is all very private, but I wished you to know what was going on. Send me as much advice as you like—I'll use it if I can. I wish I could see you for a good talk, Marmee. Love and trust me.

Ever your

Amy

9

TENDER TROUBLES

"JO, I'M WORRIED ABOUT BETH. I'm sure there is something on her mind, and I want you to discover what it is."

"What makes you think so, Mother?"

"I found her crying over the babies the other day. When she sings, the songs are always sad ones, and now and then I see a look in her face that I don't understand. This isn't like Beth."

After sewing thoughtfully for a minute, Jo said, "I think she is growing up, and so begins to dream dreams, and have hopes and fears and fidgets, without knowing why. Mother, Beth's eighteen, but we don't realize it, and treat her like a child, forgetting she's a woman."

"How fast you do grow up," returned her mother with a sigh and a smile.

"It can't be helped, Marmee, so you must let your birds hop out of the nest, one by one. I promise never to hop very far, if that is any comfort."

"It is a great comfort, Jo. Beth is too feeble and Amy too young to depend upon, but when the tug comes, you are always ready."

"Why, you know I don't mind hard jobs much, and there must always be one scrub in a family. Amy is splendid in fine works and I'm not, but I feel in my element when all the carpets are to be taken up, or half the family falls sick at once."

"I leave Beth to your hands, then, for she will open her tender little heart to her Jo sooner than to anyone else. If she only would get strong and cheerful again."

As she scribbled one afternoon, Jo kept her eye on her sister, who seemed unusually quiet. Sitting at the window, Beth's work often dropped into her lap, and she leaned her head upon her hand, in a dejected attitude, while her eyes rested on the dull, autumnal landscape. Suddenly someone familiar passed below, whistling like an operatic blackbird.

Beth started, leaned forward, smiled and nodded, watched the passerby till his quick tramp died away, then said softly as if to herself, "How strong and well and happy that dear boy looks."

"Hum!" said Jo, still intent upon her sister's face, for the bright color faded as quickly as it came, the smile vanished, and presently a tear lay shining on the window ledge. Jo saw Beth's hand go quietly to her eyes more than once, and in her half-averted face read a tender sorrow that made her own eyes fill. She slipped away, murmuring something about needing more paper.

"Mercy on me, Beth loves Laurie!" she said, sitting down in her own room, pale with the shock of the discovery which she believed she had just made. "I never dreamed of such a thing. What will Mother say? I wonder if he . . ." There Jo stopped and turned scarlet with a sudden thought. "If he shouldn't love back again, how dreadful it would be. He must. I'll make him!" And she shook her head threateningly at the picture of the mischievous-looking boy laughing at her from the wall. "Oh dear, we are growing up with a vengeance. Here's Meg married and a mamma, Amy flourishing away at Paris, and Beth in love. I'm the only one that has sense enough to keep out of mischief."

Though Laurie flirted with Amy and joked with Jo, his manner to Beth had always been peculiarly kind and gentle, but so was everybody's. Therefore, no one thought of imagining that he cared more

Beth . . . watched the passerby till his quick tramp died away.

for her than for the others. Indeed, a general impression had prevailed in the family of late that "our boy" was getting fonder than ever of Jo, who, however, wouldn't hear a word upon the subject and scolded violently if anyone dared to suggest it.

When Laurie first went to college, he fell in love about once a month. But there came a time when Laurie ceased to worship at many shrines, hinted darkly at one all-absorbing passion, and indulged occasionally in fits of gloom. Then he avoided the tender subject altogether, turned studious, and gave out that he intended to graduate in a blaze of glory. This suited Jo for she preferred imaginary heroes to real ones.

If she had not got the new idea into her head, Jo would have seen nothing unusual in the fact that Beth was very quiet that night, and Laurie very kind to her. But her imagination galloped away with her at a great pace, and common sense did not come to the rescue. As usual Beth lay on the sofa and Laurie sat in a low chair close by, amusing her with all sorts of news. But that evening Jo fancied that Beth's eyes rested on the lively, dark face beside her with peculiar pleasure, and that she listened with intense interest to an account of some exciting cricket match, though the phrases, "caught off a tice," "stumped off his ground," and "the leg hit for three," were as intelligible to her as Sanskrit. She also fancied, having set her heart upon seeing it, that she saw a certain increase of gentleness in Laurie's manner.

"Who knows? Stranger things have happened," thought Jo, as she fussed about the room. "She will make an angel of him, and he will make life delightfully easy and pleasant for the dear, if they only love each other. I don't see how he can help it, and I do believe he would if I were out of the way."

Now, the old sofa was a regular patriarch of a sofa—long, broad, well-cushioned, low, and a trifle shabby, as well it might be, for the girls had slept and sprawled on it as babies, fished over the back, rode on the arms, and had menageries under it as children, and rested tired heads, dreamed dreams, and listened to tender talk on it as young women. They all loved it, for it was a family refuge, and one corner had always been Jo's favorite lounging place. Among the many pillows that adorned the venerable couch was one, hard, round, covered with prickly horsehair, and furnished with a knobby button at each end. This repulsive pillow was her special property, being used as a weapon of defense, a barricade, or a stern preventive of too much slumber.

Laurie knew this pillow well, and had cause to regard it with deep aversion, having been unmercifully pummeled with it in former days when romping was allowed, and now frequently prevented by it from taking the seat he most coveted next to Jo in the sofa corner. If "the sausage," as they called it, stood on end, it was a sign that he might come close. But if it lay flat across the sofa, woe to the man, woman, or child who dared disturb it! That evening Jo forgot to barricade her corner and had not been in her seat five minutes before a massive form appeared beside her, and, with both arms spread over the sofa back, both long legs stretched out before him, Laurie sighed with satisfaction.

· Jo slammed down the pillow. But it was too late, there was no room for it, and coasting onto the floor, it disappeared in a most mysterious manner.

"Come, Jo, don't be thorny. After studying himself to a skeleton all the week, a fellow deserves pampering and ought to get it."

"Beth will pamper you, I'm busy."

"No, she's not to be bothered with me. But you like that sort of thing, unless you've suddenly lost your taste for it. Have you? Do you hate your boy and want to fire pillows at him?"

Anything more wheedlesome than that touching appeal was seldom heard, but Jo quenched "her boy" by turning on him with the stern query, "How many bouquets have you sent Miss Randal this week?"

"Not one, upon my word. She's engaged. Now then."

"I'm glad of it, that's one of your foolish extravagances—sending flowers and things to girls for whom you don't care two pins."

"Sensible girls for whom I do care whole papers of pins won't let me send them 'flowers and things,' so what can I do?"

"Mother doesn't approve of flirting even in fun, and you do flirt desperately, Teddy."

"I'd give anything if I could answer, 'So do you.' As I can't, I'll merely say that I don't see any harm in that pleasant little game, if all parties understand that it's only play."

"Well, it does look pleasant, but I can't learn how it's done," said Jo.

"Take lessons of Amy, she has a regular talent for it."

"Yes, she does it prettily. I suppose it's natural to some people to please without trying, and others to always say and do the wrong thing in the wrong place."

"I'm glad you can't flirt. It's refreshing to see a sensible, straight-forward girl, who can be jolly and kind without making a fool of herself. Between ourselves, Jo, some of the girls I know don't mean any harm, I'm sure, but if they knew how we fellows talked about them afterward, they'd mend their ways, I fancy."

"The girls do the same, and as their tongues are the sharpest, you fellows get the worst of it, for you are as silly as they, every bit." Jo knew that "young Laurence" was regarded as most eligible by worldly mammas, was much smiled upon by their daughters, and flattered enough by ladies of all ages to make him conceited. Dropping her voice, she said, "Teddy, go and devote yourself to one of the 'pretty, modest girls' whom you do respect, and don't waste your time with the silly ones."

"You really advise it?" And Laurie looked at her with an odd mixture of anxiety and merriment in his face.

"Yes, I do. But you'd better wait till you are through in college, on the whole, and be fitting yourself for the place meantime. You're not half good enough for . . . well, whoever the modest girl may be." The name Beth had almost escaped her.

"That I'm not!" acquiesced Laurie, with an expression of humility quite new to him, as he dropped his eyes and absently wound Jo's apron tassel round his finger.

"Mercy on us, this will never do," thought Jo, adding aloud, "Go and sing to me. I'm dying for some music, and always like yours."

"I'd rather stay here, thank you."

"Well, you can't, there isn't room. Go and make yourself useful, since you are too big to be ornamental. I thought you hated to be tied to a woman's apron string," retorted Jo, quoting certain rebellious words of his own.

"Ah, that depends on who wears the apron!" and Laurie gave an audacious tweak at the tassel.

"Are you going?" demanded Jo, diving for the pillow.

He fled the room at once, and the minute he began to sing, she slipped away to return no more till he had angrily departed.

Jo lay long awake that night, and was just dropping off when the sound of a stifled sob made her fly to Beth's bedside, with the anxious inquiry, "What is it, dear?"

"I thought you were asleep," sobbed Beth.

"Is it the old pain, my precious?"

"No, it's a new one, but I can bear it." And Beth tried to check her tears.

"Tell me all about it, and let me cure it."

"You can't, there is no cure." There Beth's voice gave way, and clinging to her sister, she cried so despairingly that Jo was frightened.

As her hand went softly to and fro across Beth's hot forehead and wet eyelids, her heart was full and she longed to speak. But young as she was, Jo had learned that hearts, like flowers, cannot be rudely handled, but must open naturally. So though she believed she knew the cause of Beth's new pain, she only said, in her tenderest tone, "Does anything trouble you, deary?"

"Yes, Jo," after a long pause.

"Wouldn't it comfort you to tell me what it is?"

"Not now, not yet. I'll tell you by-and-by."

"Is the pain better now?"

"Oh, yes, much better, you are so comforting, Jo!"

On the morrow Beth seemed herself again, for at eighteen neither heads nor hearts ache long, and a loving word can cure most ills.

But Jo had made up her mind, and after pondering over a project for some days, she confided it to her Mother. "I want to go away somewhere this winter for a change."

"Why, Jo?" And her mother looked up quickly, as if the words suggested a double meaning.

With her eyes on her work Jo answered soberly, "I had a bright idea yesterday, and this is it. You know Mrs. Kirke wrote to you for some respectable young person to teach her children and sew. I think I should suit if I tried."

"My dear, go out to service in that great boardinghouse in New York?" And Mrs. March looked surprised, but not displeased.

"Mrs. Kirke is your friend—the kindest soul that ever lived—and would make things pleasant for me, I know. It's honest work, and I'm not ashamed of it."

"Nor I. But your writing?"

"All the better for the change. I shall see and hear new things, get new ideas, and, even if I haven't much time there, I shall bring home quantities of material for my rubbish."

"I have no doubt of it, but are these your only reasons for this sudden fancy? May I know the others?"

Jo looked up and Jo looked down, then said slowly, with sudden color in her cheeks, "It may be vain and wrong to say it, but . . . I'm afraid . . . Laurie is getting too fond of me."

"Then you don't care for him in the way it is evident he begins to care for you?" And Mrs. March looked anxious as she put the question.

"Mercy, no! I love the dear boy, as I always have, and am immensely proud of him, but as for anything more, it's out of the question."

"I'm glad, dear, because I don't think you are suited to one another. As friends you are happy, and your frequent quarrels soon blow over, but I fear you would both rebel if you were mated for life. You are too much alike and too fond of freedom, not to mention hot tempers and strong wills, to get on happily together in a relation which needs infinite patience and forbearance, as well as love."

"That's just the feeling I had, though I couldn't express it. I'm glad you think he is only beginning to care for me. It would trouble me sadly to make him unhappy, for I couldn't fall in love with the dear old fellow merely out of gratitude, could I?" The color deepened in Jo's cheeks, with the look of mingled pleasure, pride, and pain which young girls wear when speaking of first lovers.

"If it can be managed you shall go. Mothers may differ in their management, but the hope is the same in all—the desire to see their children happy. Meg is so, and I am content. You I leave to enjoy your liberty till you tire of it, for only then will you find that there is something sweeter. Amy is my chief care now, but her good sense will help her. For Beth, I indulge no hopes except that she may be well. By the way, have you spoken to her?"

"Yes, she owned she had a trouble, and promised to tell me by-and-by. I said no more, for I think I know it." And Jo told her little story. But Mrs. March shook her head and did not take so romantic a view of the case.

Jo could not rid herself of the foreboding fear that Laurie would not get over his "lovelornity" as easily as before. When all was settled, with fear and trembling she told him, but to her surprise he took it quietly. He had been graver than usual of late, but pleasant, and when jokingly accused of turning over a new leaf, he answered soberly, "So I am, and I mean this one shall stay turned."

Jo, much relieved that one of his virtuous fits should come on just then, made her preparations with a lightened heart—for Beth seemed more cheerful—and hoped she was doing the best for all.

"One thing I leave to your special care," she said, the night before she left.

"You mean your papers?" asked Beth.

"No—my boy. Be good to him, won't you?"

"Of course I will, but I can't fill your place, and he'll miss you sadly."

"It won't hurt him. So remember, I leave him in your charge, to plague, pamper, and keep in order."

"I'll do my best, for your sake," promised Beth, wondering why Jo looked at her so strangely.

When Laurie said goodbye, he whispered significantly, "It won't do a bit of good, Jo. My eye is on you, so mind what you do, or I'll come and bring you home."

10
JO'S JOURNAL

Dear Marmee and Beth,

I'm going to write you a regular volume, for I've got heaps to tell, though I'm not a fine young lady traveling around Europe. When I lost sight of Father's dear old face, I felt a trifle blue and might have shed a tear or two if an Irish lady with four small children, all crying more or less, hadn't diverted my mind. I amused myself by dropping gingerbread nuts over the seat every time they opened their mouths to roar.

Soon the sun came out, and taking it as a good omen, I cleared up likewise and enjoyed my journey with all my heart.

Mrs. Kirke welcomed me so kindly I felt at home at once, even in that big house full of strangers. She gave me a funny little sky parlor with a nice table in a sunny window, so I can sit here and write whenever I like. A fine view and a church tower opposite atone for the many stairs. The nursery, where I am to teach and sew, is a pleasant room next to Mrs. Kirke's private parlor, and the two little girls are pretty children, rather spoiled, I fancy, but they took to me after telling them The Seven Bad Pigs, and I've no doubt I shall make a model governess. I can have my meals with the children, or with the boarders.

"Now, my dear, make yourself at home," said Mrs. K. in her motherly way. "A great anxiety will be off my mind if I know the children are safe with you. There are some pleasant people in the house if you feel sociable, and your evenings are always free. Come to me if anything goes wrong, and be as happy as you can. There's the tea bell, I must run." And off she bustled, leaving me to settle myself in my new nest.

As I went downstairs soon after, I saw something I liked. The flights are long in this tall house, and as I stood waiting at the head of the third one for a little servant girl to lumber up, I saw a gentleman come along behind her, take the heavy coal out of her hand, carry it all the way up, put it down at a door near by, and walk away, saying, with a kind nod and a foreign accent, "It goes better so. The little back is too young to haf such heaviness."

When I mentioned it to Mrs. K. that evening, she laughed, and said, "That must have been Professor Bhaer. He's always doing things of that sort." She told me he was from Berlin, very learned and good, but poor as a church mouse. He gives lessons to support himself and two little orphan nephews he is educating here, according to the wishes of his sister, who married an American. Mrs. K. lends him her parlor for some of his scholars. There is a glass door between it and the nursery, and I mean to peep at him, and then I'll tell you how he looks. He's almost forty, so it's no harm, Marmee.

After tea and a go-to-bed romp with the little girls, I attacked the big workbasket, and had a quiet evening chatting with Mrs. K. I shall keep a journal-letter and send it once a week, so good night, and more tomorrow.

Tuesday Eve

Had a lively time this morning, for the children were wild, and at one time I thought I should shake them. Some good angel inspired me to try gymnastics, and I kept it up till they were glad to sit down and keep still. After luncheon, the girl took them out for a walk, and I started on my needlework. I was thanking my stars that I'd learned to make nice buttonholes, when the parlor door opened and shut, and someone began to hum like a big bumblebee.

It was dreadfully improper, I know, but I couldn't resist the temptation, and lifting one end of the curtain, I peeped in. Professor Bhaer was there, and while he arranged his books, I took a good look at him. A regular German—stout, with brown hair tumbled all over his head, a bushy beard, good nose, and the kindest eyes I ever saw. He looked sober in spite of his humming, till he went to the window to turn the hyacinth bulbs toward the sun, and stroked the cat, who received him like an old friend. Then he smiled, and when a tap came at the door, called out in a loud, brisk tone, "Herein!"

I was just going to run, when I caught sight of a morsel of a child carrying a big book, and stopped to see what was going on.

"Me wants my Bhaer," said the mite, slamming down her book and running to meet him.

"You shall haf your Bhaer. Come, then, and take a goot hug from him, my Tina," said the Professor, catching her up with a laugh, and holding her so high over his head that she had to stoop her little face to kiss him.

"Now me mus tuddy my lessin," went on the funny little thing. So he put her up at the table, opened the great dictionary she had brought, and gave her a paper and pencil. She scribbled away, turning a leaf now and then, and passing her little fat finger down the page, as if finding a word, so soberly that I nearly betrayed myself by a laugh. Mr. Bhaer stood stroking her pretty hair with a fatherly look that made me think she must be his own.

Another knock and the appearance of two young ladies sent me back to my work, and there I virtuously remained through all the noise and gabbing that went on next door. One of the girls kept laughing affectedly, and saying "Now Professor," and the other pronounced her German with an accent that must have made it hard for him to keep sober.

More than once I heard him say emphatically, "No, no, it is not so, you haf not attend to what I say," and once there was a loud rap, as if he struck the table with his book, followed by the despairing exclamation, "Prut! It all goes bad this day."

When the girls were gone, I took just one more peep to see if he survived it. He seemed to have thrown himself back in his chair, tired out, and sat there with his eyes shut till the clock struck two, when he jumped up, put his books in his pocket, as if ready for another lesson, and, taking in his arms little Tina who had fallen asleep on the sofa, he carried her quietly away.

Mrs. Kirke asked me if I wouldn't go down to the five o'clock dinner, and feeling a little bit homesick, I thought I would, just to see what sort of people are under the same roof with me. She gave me a seat by her, and after my face cooled off, I plucked up courage and looked about me. There was the usual assortment of young men absorbed in themselves, young couples absorbed in each other, married ladies in their babies, and old gentlemen in politics. I don't think I shall care to have much to do with any of them, except one sweet-faced maiden lady.

Cast away at the end of the table was the Professor, shouting answers to the questions of a deaf old gentleman on one side, and talking philosophy with a Frenchman on the other. He had a great appetite, and shoveled in his dinner in a manner which would have horrified Amy. I didn't mind, for I like "to see folks eat with a relish," as Hannah says, and the poor man must have needed a deal of food after teaching idiots all day.

As I went upstairs after dinner, two of the young men were putting on their hats before the hall mirror, and I heard one say low to the other, "Who's the new party?"

"Governess, or something of that sort."

"Handsome head, but no style."

"Not a bit of it. Give us a light and come on."

I felt angry at first, but I've got sense, if I haven't style, which is more than some people have, judging from the remarks of these elegant beings who clattered away, smoking like bad chimneys. I hate ordinary people!

Thursday

Yesterday was a quiet day spent teaching, sewing, and writing in my little room, which is cozy with its light and fire. I was introduced to the Professor. It seems that Tina is the child of the Frenchwoman who does the fine ironing in the laundry here. The little thing has lost her heart to Mr. Bhaer, and follows him about the house like a dog whenever he is at home, which delights him. Kitty and Minnie Kirke tell all sorts of stories about the plays he invents, the presents he brings, and the splendid tales he tells. The young men quiz him, call him Old Fritz, and make all manner of jokes on his name. But he enjoys it like a boy, Mrs. K. says, and takes it so good-naturedly that they all like him in spite of his foreign ways.

The maiden lady is a Miss Norton—rich, cultivated, and kind. She spoke to me at dinner today (for I went to table again, it's such fun to watch people), and asked me to come and see her at her room. She has fine books and pictures and seems friendly, so I shall make myself agreeable, for I do want to get into good society, only it isn't the same sort that Amy likes.

I was in our parlor last evening when Mr. Bhaer came in with some newspapers for Mrs. Kirke. She wasn't there, but Minnie introduced me prettily: "This is Mamma's friend, Miss March."

"Yes, and she's jolly and we like her lots," added Kitty.

We both bowed, and then we laughed, for the prim introduction and the blunt addition were a comical contrast.

"Ah, yes, I hear these naughty ones go to vex you, Mees Marsch. If so again, call at me and I come," he said, with a threatening frown that delighted the little wretches.

Today as I passed his door on my way out, by accident I knocked against it with my umbrella. It flew open, and there he stood in his robe, with a big blue sock on one hand and a darning needle in the other. He didn't seem at all ashamed of it, for when I explained and hurried on, he waved his hand, sock and all, saying in his loud, cheerful way, "You haf a fine day to make your walk. Bon voyage, mademoiselle."

I laughed all the way downstairs, but it was a little pathetic, also to think of the poor man having to mend his own clothes.

Saturday

Nothing has happened to write about, except a call on Miss Norton, who showed me all her treasures, and asked me if I would sometimes go with her to lectures and concerts. She put it as a favor, but I'm sure she does it out of kindness. I'm as proud as Lucifer, but such favors from such people don't burden me, and I accepted gratefully.

When I got back to the nursery there was such an uproar in the parlor that I looked in, and there was Mr. Bhaer down on his hands and knees, with Tina on his back, Kitty leading him with a jump rope, and Minnie feeding two small boys with seedcakes, as they roared and ramped in cages built of chairs.

"We are playing zoo," explained Kitty.

"Dis is mine effalunt!" added Tina, holding on by the Professor's hair.

"Mamma always allows us to do what we like Saturday afternoon, when Franz and Emil come, doesn't she, Mr. Bhaer?" said Minnie.

The "effalunt" sat up and said soberly to me, "If we make too large a noise you shall say hush to us, and we go more softly."

I left the door open and enjoyed the fun as much as they did. They played tag and soldiers, danced and sang, and when it began to grow dark they all piled onto the sofa about the Professor, while he told charming fairy stories.

Forward Amy's letters as soon as you can spare them. My small news will sound flat after her splendors. Is Teddy studying so hard that he can't find time to write to his friends? Take good care of him for me, Beth, and tell me all about the babies, and give heaps of love to everyone.

From your faithful

Jo

P.S. On reading over my letter it strikes me as rather Bhaery, but I am always interested in odd people. Bless you!

December

My Precious Betsey,

As this is to be a scribble-scrabble letter, I direct it to you, for it may amuse you, and give you some idea of my goings on. Franz and Emil are jolly little lads, quite after my own heart, for the mixture of German and American spirit in them produces a constant state of effervescence. Saturday afternoons are riotous times. On pleasant days the children all go walking, with the Professor and myself to keep order, and then such fun!

We are good friends now, and I've begun to take German lessons. I couldn't help it. To begin at the beginning, Mrs. Kirke called to me one day as I passed Mr. Bhaer's room where she was rummaging.

"Did you ever see such a den, my dear? Just come and help me put these books to rights, for I've turned everything upside down, trying to discover what he has done with the six new handkerchiefs I gave him."

Books and papers were everywhere, and a box of white mice sat on the window seat; half-finished boats and bits of string lay among the manuscripts; dirty little boots stood drying before the fire; and traces of the dearly beloved boys, for whom he makes a slave of himself, were all over the room. After a grand rummage, three of the missing articles were found—one over the bird cage, one covered with ink, and a third burned brown, having been used as a hotpad.

"Such a man!" laughed good-natured Mrs. K. "I suppose the others are torn up to rig ships, bandage cut fingers, or make kite tails. It's dreadful, but I can't scold him. He's so absent-minded and good-natured, he lets those boys ride over him roughshod. I agreed to do his washing and mending, but he forgets to give out his things, so he comes to a sad pass sometimes."

"Let me mend them," I said. "I don't mind it, and he needn't know. I'd like to—he's so kind to me about bringing my letters and lending books."

So I knit heels into two pairs of the socks—for they were boggled out of shape with his unusual darns. I hoped he wouldn't find it out, but one day last week he caught me at it. Tina runs in and out, leaving the door open, and I can hear his lessons. I had been sitting near this door, finishing off the last sock, and trying to understand what he said to a new scholar, who is as stupid as I am. The girl had gone, and I thought he had also, it was so still, and I was busily gabbling over a verb, and rocking to and fro in a most absurd way, when I looked up, and there was Mr. Bhaer.

"So!" he said, as I stopped and stared like a goose, "you peep at me, I peep at you, and that is not bad. But see, I am not pleasanting when I say, haf you a wish for German?"

"Yes, but you are too busy. I am too stupid to learn," I blundered.

"Prut! we will make the time, and we fail not to find the sense. At efening I shall gif a little lesson with much gladness, for, look you, Mees Marsch, I haf this debt to pay." And he pointed to my work. "'Yes,' they say to one another, these so kind ladies, 'he is a stupid old fellow, he will see not what we do, he will never opserve that his sock heels go not in holes any more, he will think his buttons grow out new when they fall.' Ah! But I haf an eye, and I see much. I haf a heart, and I feel the thanks for this. Come, a little lesson then and now, or no more good fairy works for me and mine."

I made the bargain, and we began. I took four lessons, and then I stuck fast in a grammatical bog. The Professor was patient with me, but it must have been torment to him, he'd look at me with such an expression of mild despair that it was a toss-up with me whether to laugh or cry. When I sniffed with utter woe, he just threw the grammar on to the floor and marched out of the room. I felt myself disgraced and deserted forever and was scrambling my papers together, meaning to rush upstairs, when in he came, brisk and beaming.

"Now we shall try a new way. You and I will read these pleasant little stories together, and dig no more in that dry book, that goes in the corner for making us trouble."

He spoke so kindly, and opened Hans Andersen's fairy tales so invitingly before me, that I forgot my bashfulness and went at it with all my might, tumbling over long words, pronouncing according to the inspiration of the minute, and doing my best. When I stopped for breath, he clapped his hands and cried out, in his hearty way, "*Das ist gut!* Now we go well! My turn. I do him in German, gif me your ear." And away he went, rumbling out the words with relish. Fortunately the story was the *Faithful Tin Soldier*, which is droll, you know, so I could laugh—and I did—though I didn't understand half of what he read.

After that we got on better, and now I read my lessons pretty well, for this way of studying suits me, and the grammar gets tucked into the tales and poetry like swallowing pills with jelly. I like it very much, and he doesn't seem tired of it yet—which is good of him, isn't it?

I'm glad Laurie seems so happy and busy, that he has given up smoking and lets his hair grow. You manage him better than I did. I'm not jealous, dear, do your best, only don't make a saint of him. I'm afraid I couldn't like him without a spice of human naughtiness. Read him bits of my letters. I haven't time to write much, and that will do just as well.

January

A Happy New Year to you all, my dearest family, which of course includes Mr. L. and a young man by the name of Teddy. I can't tell you how much I enjoyed your Christmas bundle, for I didn't get it till night and had given up hoping. I felt a little low as I sat up in my room after tea, and when the big, muddy, battered-looking bundle was brought to me, I just hugged it and pranced. It was so homey and refreshing that I sat down on the floor and read and looked and ate and laughed and cried. The things were just what I wanted, and all the better for being made instead of bought. Beth's new "ink bib" was capital, and Hannah's box of hard gingerbread will be a treasure. I'll be sure and wear the nice flannels you sent, Marmee, and read carefully the books Father has marked. Thank you all, heaps and heaps!

On New Year's Day Mr. Bhaer gave me a fine Shakespeare. It is one he values much, and I've often admired it, set up in the place of honor with his German Bible, Plato, Homer, and Milton. So you may imagine how I felt when he brought it down, without its cover, and showed me my name in it, "From your friend Friedrich Bhaer."

"You say often you wish a library. Here I gif you one, for between these lids (he meant covers) is many books in one. Read him well, and he will help you much, for the study of character in this book will help you to read it in the world and paint it with your pen."

I thanked him as well as I could, and talk now about "my library," as if I had a hundred books. I never knew how much there was in Shakespeare before, but then I never had a Bhaer to explain it to me. Now don't laugh at his name. It isn't pronounced either Bear or Beer, but something between the two. Mother would admire his warm heart, Father his wise head.

Not having much money, or knowing what he'd like, I got several little things, and put them about the room, where he would find them unexpectedly. They were all useful, pretty, or funny.

There was a masquerade party here New Year's Eve. I didn't mean to go down, having no costume, but at the last minute, Mrs. Kirke remembered some old brocades, and Miss Norton lent me lace and feathers. So I dressed up as Mrs. Malaprop, and sailed in with a mask on. No one knew me, for I disguised my voice, and no one dreamed the silent, haughty Miss March (for they think I am stiff and cool, most of them, and so I am to whippersnappers) could dance and dress and play a part.

I enjoyed it very much, and when we unmasked it was fun to see them stare at me. I heard one of the young men tell another that he knew I'd been an actress—he thought he remembered seeing me on stage.

I had a happy New Year, after all, and when I thought it over in my room, I felt as if I was getting on a little in spite of my many failures. I'm cheerful all the time now, work with a will, and take more interest in other people than I used to. Bless you all! Ever your loving

Jo

11
A FRIEND

Jo STILL FOUND TIME for literary labors. She saw that money means power, and she made up her mind to get money and power—not to be used for herself alone, but for those she loved.

The dream of filling home with comforts, giving Beth everything she wanted, from strawberries in winter to an organ in her bedroom, going abroad herself, and always having more than enough, so that she might indulge in the luxury of charity, had been for years Jo's most cherished castle in the air.

She told no one, but concocted a "thrilling tale," and boldly carried it herself to Mr. Dashwood, editor of the Weekly Volcano. Instinct told her that clothes are apt to influence people more than fine character or good manners. So she dressed herself in her best, and trying to persuade herself that she was neither excited nor nervous, bravely climbed two flights of dark, dirty stairs to find herself in a disorderly room, a cloud of cigar smoke, and the presence of three seated gentlemen, with their heels higher than their hats—which none of them took the trouble to remove. Somewhat daunted by this reception, Jo hesitated on the threshold, murmuring in much embarrassment, "Excuse me, I was looking for the *Weekly Volcano* office. I wished to see Mr. Dashwood."

Down went the shoes, up rose the smokiest gentleman, and carefully cherishing his cigar between his fingers, he advanced with a nod and a face full of sleep. Feeling that she must get through the matter somehow, Jo produced her manuscript, and, blushing redder and redder with each sentence, blundered out fragments of the little speech carefully prepared for the occasion.

"A friend of mine desired me to offer . . . a story . . . just as an experiment . . . would like your opinion . . . be glad to write more if you like it."

While she blushed and blundered, Mr. Dashwood had taken the manuscript, and was turning over the neat pages with a pair of dirty fingers.

"Not a first attempt, I take it?" observing that the pages were numbered and correctly covered only on one side.

"No, sir. She has had some experience, and got a prize for a tale in the *Blarneystone Banner.* "

"Oh, did she?" And Mr. Dashwood gave Jo a quick look, which seemed to take note of everything she had on, from the bow in her bonnet to the buttons on her boots. "Well, you can leave it, if you like. We've more of this sort of thing on hand than we know what to do with at present, but I'll run my eye over it, and give you an answer next week."

Now, Jo did not like to leave it, for Mr. Dashwood didn't suit her at all. But under the circumstances, there was nothing for her to do but bow and walk away, looking particularly tall and dignified, as she was apt to do when embarrassed. It was perfectly evident from the knowing glances exchanged among the gentlemen that her little fiction of "my friend" was considered a good joke, and a laugh broke out when the editor closed the door. Half resolving never to return, she went home and worked off her irritation by stitching pinafores vigorously, and in an hour or two was cool enough to laugh over the scene and long for next week.

When she went again, Mr. Dashwood was alone and much wider

awake than before, so the second interview was more comfortable than the first.

"We'll take this if you don't object to a few alterations. It's too long, but omitting the passages I've marked will make it just the right length," he said, in a businesslike tone.

Jo hardly knew her own manuscript again, so crumpled and underlined were its pages and paragraphs. But feeling as a tender parent might on being asked to cut off her baby's legs in order that it might fit into a new cradle, she looked at the marked passages and was surprised to find that all the moral lessons had been crossed out.

"But, sir, I thought every story should have some sort of a moral, so I took care to have a few of my sinners repent."

Mr. Dashwood relaxed into a smile, for Jo had forgotten her "friend," and spoken as only an author could. "People want to be amused, not preached at. Morals don't sell nowadays," which was not quite correct.

"You think it would do with these alterations, then?"

"Yes, it's an original plot, well worked up—language good, and so on."

"What do you . . . that is, what payment . . ." began Jo.

"Oh, yes, well, we give from twenty-five to thirty for things of this sort. Pay when it comes out," returned Mr. Dashwood, as if that point had escaped him.

"Very well, you can have it," said Jo, handing back the story with a satisfied air, for after a dollar a column, twenty-five seemed good pay. "Shall I tell my friend you will take another if she has a better one?"

"Well, we'll look at it. Can't promise to take it. Tell her to make it short and spicy, and never mind the moral. What name would your friend like on it?"

"None at all, if you please, she doesn't wish her name to appear and has no pen name," said Jo, blushing in spite of herself.

"Just as she likes! The tale will be out next week. Will you call for the money, or shall I send it?" asked Mr. Dashwood.

"I'll call. Good morning, sir."

As she departed, Mr. Dashwood put up his feet and remarked, "Poor and proud, but she'll do."

Like most young scribblers, she used foreign characters and scenery, and bandits, counts, gypsies, nuns, and duchesses appeared upon her stage. Her readers were not particular about such trifles as grammar, punctuation, and probability, and Mr. Dashwood graciously permitted her to fill his columns at the lowest prices.

Her little savings to take Beth to the mountains next summer grew slowly but surely as the weeks passed. It disturbed her not to tell her family, but she quieted her conscience by anticipations of the happy minute when she should show her earnings and laugh over her well-kept secret.

Mr. Dashwood rejected any but thrilling tales, and as thrills could not be produced except by frightening the souls of the readers, Jo had to ransack history and romance, land and sea, science and art, police records and lunatic asylums. Eager to find material for stories, and bent on making them original in plot, she searched newspapers for accidents and crimes. She excited the suspicions of public librarians by asking for works on poisons. She studied faces in the street, and characters, good, bad, and indifferent. She delved in the dust of ancient times for facts or fictions so old that they were as good as new, and introduced herself to folly, sin, and misery, as well as her limited opportunities allowed. She was fast gaining a premature acquaintance with the darker side of life, which comes soon enough to all of us.

While endowing her imaginary heroes with every perfection under the sun, Jo was discovering a live hero, who interested her in spite of many human imperfections. Mr. Bhaer, in one of their conversations, had advised her to study simple, true, and lovely characters, wherever she found them, as good training for a writer. Jo took him at his word, for she turned round and studied him—which would have much surprised him, had he known it.

Why everybody liked him was what puzzled Jo, at first. He was neither rich nor great, young nor handsome—in no respect what is called fascinating, imposing, or brilliant. Yet people seemed to gather about him as naturally as about a fireplace. He was poor, yet always appeared to be giving something away; a stranger, yet everyone was his friend; no longer young, but as happy-hearted as a boy; plain looking, yet his face looked beautiful to many. If he had any sorrow, "it sat with its head under its wing," and he turned only his sunny side to the world. The pleasant lines about his mouth were the memorials of many friendly words and cheery laughs, his eyes were never cold or hard, and his big hand had a warm, strong grasp.

"That's it!" said Jo to herself, when she at length discovered that genuine good will toward one's fellow men could beautify and dignify even a stout German teacher, who shoveled in his dinner, darned his own socks, and was burdened with the name of Bhaer.

Jo valued goodness highly, but she also respected intellect. He never spoke of himself, and no one ever knew that in his native city he had been much honored for his learning, till another German came to see him and mentioned it to Miss Norton. Jo felt proud that he was an honored professor in Berlin, though only a poor language-teacher in America, and for Jo this was the spice of adventure.

He had something better than intellect which Jo discovered next. Miss Norton took Jo and the Professor with her one night to a select symposium, held in honor of several celebrities.

Jo went prepared to bow down and adore the mighty ones—a famous poet, a novelist, a preacher, a philosopher, a musician, and a British nobleman. But her reverence for genius received a severe shock that night from the discovery that the great creatures were only men and women after all. Imagine her dismay at finding that every one of them had a flaw like piggishness, drinking too much, flirting, acting catty, dozing, babbling, gossiping, talking about race horses, or being dull.

Before the evening was half over, Jo sat down in a corner to recover herself and Mr. Bhaer soon joined her. Presently several philosophers came ambling up to hold an intellectual discussion. It dawned upon her gradually that they were picking the world to pieces and putting it back together on new and (they claimed) infinitely better principles. They showed that religion could be reasoned into nothingness, and intellect was to be the only God. Jo knew nothing about philosophy, but a curious excitement, half pleasurable, half painful, came over her as she listened with a sense of being turned adrift into time and space.

She looked round to see how the Professor liked it, and found him looking at her with the grimmest expression she had ever seen him wear. He shook his head and beckoned her to come away, but she was fascinated just then and kept her seat, trying to find out what the wise gentlemen intended to rely upon after they had annihilated all the old beliefs.

Mr. Bhaer bore it as long as he could, but when he was appealed to for an opinion, he blazed up with honest indignation and defended religion with all the eloquence of truth—an eloquence which made his broken English musical and his plain face beautiful. Somehow, as he talked, the world got right again to Jo. The old beliefs, that had lasted so long, seemed better than the new. God was not a blind force, and immortality was not a pretty fable, but a blessed fact. She felt as if she had solid ground under her feet again, and when Mr. Bhaer paused, she wanted to clap her hands and thank him.

Jo began to see that character is a better possession than money, rank, intellect, or beauty. This belief strengthened daily. She wanted to be worthy of Mr. Bhaer's friendship, and just when the wish was sincerest, she came near losing everything. It all grew out of a cocked hat, for one evening the Professor came in to give Jo her lesson with a paper soldier cap on his head, which Tina had put there and he had forgotten to take off.

"It's evident he doesn't look in his mirror before coming down," thought Jo, with a smile, as he said, "Goot efening," and sat soberly down. She liked to hear his big, hearty laugh when anything funny happened, so she left him to discover it for himself. After the reading came the lesson, which was a lively one, for Jo was in a gay mood that night, and the cocked hat kept her eyes dancing with merriment. The Professor didn't know what to make of her, and stopped at last to ask, "Mees Marsch, for what do you laugh in your master's face? Haf you no respect for me?"

"How can I be respectful, sir, when you forget to take your hat off?"

Lifting his hand to his head, the absent-minded Professor gravely felt and removed the newspaper hat, looked at it a minute, and then threw back his head and laughed like a merry bass viol.

"Ah! I see him now, it is that imp Tina who makes me a fool with my cap. Well, if this lesson goes not well, you too shall wear him."

Then Mr. Bhaer caught sight of a picture on the hat, and unfolding it, said with an air of great disgust, "I wish these papers did not come in the house, they are not for children to see, nor young people to read. I haf no patience with those who make this harm."

Jo glanced at the sheet and saw a lunatic, a corpse, a villain, and a viper. For a minute she fancied the paper was the *Volcano*. It was not, and even if it had been, with one of her own tales in it, there would have been no name to betray her. Her face betrayed her, however. The Professor had wondered what Jo wrote. Now it occurred to him that she was ashamed of her writing.

She answered, "All may not be bad, only silly, you know. Many respectable people make an honest living out of violent adventure stories."

"There is a demand for whisky, but I think you and I do not care to sell it. If the respectable people knew what harm they did, they would not feel that the living was honest. They haf no right to put poison in the sugarplum, and let the small ones eat it. No, they should think a little, and sweep mud in the street before they do this thing." Mr. Bhaer walked to the fire, crumpling the paper in his hands. Jo's cheeks burned long after the cocked hat had turned to smoke and gone harmlessly up the chimney.

"I should like much to send all the rest after him," muttered the Professor, coming back with a relieved air.

Jo thought consolingly to herself, "Mine are not like that, they are only silly, never bad, so I won't be worried." Taking up her book, she said, with a studious face, "Shall we go on, sir? I'll be good and proper now."

"I shall hope so," was all he said, but he meant more than she imagined, and the grave, kind look he gave her made her feel as if the words *Weekly Volcano* were printed in large type on her forehead.

As soon as she went to her room, she got out her papers, and carefully reread every one of her stories. They filled her with dismay.

"They are trash, and will soon be worse than trash if I go on, for each is more violent than the last. I can't read this stuff without being horribly ashamed of it, and what should I do if they were seen at home or Mr. Bhaer got hold of them?"

Jo stuffed the whole bundle into her stove, nearly setting the chimney afire with the blaze.

When nothing remained of all her three months' work except a heap of ashes and the money in her lap, Jo looked sober, as she sat on the floor, wondering what she ought to do about her wages.

"I think I haven't done much harm yet, and may keep this to pay for my time," she said, adding impatiently, "I almost wish I hadn't any conscience, it's so inconvenient. If I didn't care about doing right, and didn't feel uncomfortable when doing wrong, I should get on just fine. I can't help wishing sometimes, that Father and Mother hadn't been so particular about such things."

Jo wrote no more violent stories, but went to the other extreme and produced a tale which might have been more properly called a sermon, so intensely moral was it. She sent this gem to several markets, but it found no purchaser, and she was inclined to agree with Mr. Dashwood that morals didn't sell.

Then she tried a child's story, but the only person who offered enough to make it worth her while was a worthy gentleman who felt it his mission to convert all the world to his particular belief. As much as she liked to write for children, Jo refused to depict all her naughty boys as being eaten by bears or tossed by mad bulls because they did not go to a particular Sunday school, and the children who did go there as rewarded by every kind of bliss. So nothing came of these trials, and Jo set aside her inkstand, and said in a fit of wholesome humility, "I don't know anything. I'll wait till I do before I try again, and, meantime, 'sweep mud in the street.' That's honest, at least."

If she sometimes looked serious or a little sad no one observed it but Professor Bhaer. Jo never knew he was watching to see if she would accept and profit by his advice. But she stood the test, and he knew she had given up writing. Not only did he guess it by the fact that the second finger of her right hand was no longer inky, but she spent her evenings downstairs now, and studied hard, which assured him that she was bent on occupying her mind with something useful.

He helped her in many ways, proving himself a true friend, and Jo was happy, for while her pen lay idle, she was learning other lessons besides German, and laying a foundation for the "thrilling" story of her own life.

Jo did not leave Mrs. Kirke till June. Everyone seemed sorry when the time came. The children were inconsolable, and Mr. Bhaer's hair stuck straight up all over his head, for he always rumpled it wildly when disturbed in mind.

She bade her friends all goodbye one by one. When his turn came, she said warmly, "Now, sir, you won't forget to come and see us, if you ever travel our way, will you? I'll never forgive you if you do, for I want them all to know my friend."

"Do you? Shall I come?" he asked, looking down at her with an eager expression which she did not see.

"Yes, come next month. Laurie graduates then, and you'd enjoy Commencement as something new."

"That is your best friend, of whom you speak?" he said in an altered tone.

"Yes, my boy Teddy. I'm proud of him and should like you to see him."

Something in Mr. Bhaer's face suddenly reminded Jo that she might find Laurie more than a "best friend," and simply because she wished not to look as if anything was the matter, she began to blush, and the more she tried not to, the redder she grew. The Professor's face lost its eager look, as he said cordially, "I fear I shall not make the time for that, but I wish the friend much success, and you all happiness. Gott bless you!" And with that, he shook hands warmly, shouldered Tina, and went away.

But after the boys were in bed, he sat long before his fire with the tired look on his face and homesickness lying heavy at his heart. "It is not for me, I must not hope it now," he said to himself, with a sigh that was almost a groan. Then he went and kissed the two tousled heads upon the pillow.

Early as it was, he was at the station next morning to see Jo off. Thanks to him, she began her solitary journey with the pleasant memory of a familiar face smiling its farewell, a bunch of violets to keep her company, and, best of all, the happy thought, "Well, the winter's gone, and I've written no books, earned no fortune, but I've made a friend worth having and I'll try to keep him all my life."

12
HEARTACHE

WHATEVER HIS MOTIVE MIGHT HAVE BEEN, Laurie studied hard that year, for he graduated with honors. They were all there, his grandfather—oh, so proud!—Mr. and Mrs. March, John and Meg, Jo and Beth, and all exulted over him with the sincere admiration which boys make light of at the time, but which nothing ever matches.

"I've got to stay for this confounded supper, but I shall be home early tomorrow. You'll come and meet me as usual, girls?" Laurie said, as he put the sisters into the carriage. He said "girls," but he meant Jo, for she was the only one who kept up the old custom. She had not the heart to refuse her splendid, successful boy anything, and answered warmly, "I'll come, Teddy, rain or shine, and march before you, playing 'Hail the conquering hero comes' on a Jew's-harp."

Laurie thanked her with a look that made her think in a sudden panic, "Oh, deary me! I know he'll say something, and then what shall I do?"

Evening meditation and morning work somewhat allayed her fears, and having decided that she wouldn't be vain enough to think people were going to propose when she had given them every reason to know what her answer would be, she set forth at the appointed time. When she saw a stalwart figure looming in the distance, she had a strong desire to turn about and run away.

"Where's the Jew's-harp, Jo?" cried Laurie, as soon as he was within speaking distance.

"I forgot it." He talked on rapidly about all sorts of faraway subjects, till they turned from the road into the little path that led homeward through the grove. Then he walked more slowly, suddenly lost his fine flow of language, and now and then a dreadful pause occurred. To rescue the conversation from one of the wells of silence into which it kept falling, Jo said hastily, "Now you must have a good long holiday!"

"I intend to."

Something in his resolute tone made Jo look up quickly to find him looking down at her with an expression that assured her the dreaded moment had come, and made her put out her hand with an imploring, "No, Teddy, please don't!"

"I will, and you must hear me. It's no use, Jo, we've got to have it out, and the sooner the better for both of us," he answered, getting flushed and excited all at once.

"Say what you like, then. I'll listen," said Jo, with a desperate sort of patience.

"I've loved you ever since I've known you, Jo. I couldn't help it, you've been so good to me. I've tried to show it, but you wouldn't let me. Now I'm going to make you hear, and give me an answer, for I can't go on so any longer."

"I wanted to save you this. I thought you'd understand . . ." began Jo, finding it a great deal harder than she expected.

"I know you did, but girls are so strange you never know what they mean. They say no when they mean yes, and drive a man out of his wits just for the fun of it," returned Laurie, entrenching himself behind an undeniable fact.

"*I* don't. I never wanted to make you care for me so, and I went away to keep you from it if I could."

"I thought so. It was like you, but it was no use. I only loved you all the more, and I worked hard to please you, and I gave up billiards and everything you didn't like, and waited and never complained, for I hoped you'd love me, though I'm not half good enough." Here there was a choke that couldn't be controlled, and he caught her by the hands.

"You are, you're a great deal too good for me," said Jo. "I'm so grateful to you, and so proud and fond of you, I don't see why I can't love you as you want me to. I've tried, but I can't change the feeling, and it would be a lie to say I do when I don't."

They were in the grove now, close by the stile. When the last words fell reluctantly from Jo's lips, Laurie dropped her hands and turned as if to go. But for once in his life that fence was too much for him, so he just laid his head down on the mossy post, and stood so still that Jo was frightened.

"Oh, Teddy, I'm sorry, so desperately sorry. I could kill myself if it would do any good! I wish you wouldn't take it so hard. I can't help it. You know it's impossible for people to make themselves love other people if they don't," cried Jo remorsefully, as she softly patted his shoulder.

"They do sometimes," said a muffled voice from the post.

"I don't believe it's the right sort of love, and I'd rather not try it."

There was a long pause, while a blackbird sung blithely on the willow by the river, and the tall grass rustled in the wind. Presently Jo said soberly, as she sat down on the step of the stile, "Laurie, I want to tell you something."

He started as if he had been shot, threw up his head, and cried out in a fierce tone, "Don't tell me that, Jo, not that you love that old man!"

"What old man?" demanded Jo, thinking he must mean his grandfather.

"That devilish Professor you were always writing about. If you say you love him, I know I shall do something desperate." And he looked as if he would keep his word.

Jo started to laugh, but restrained herself and said warmly, "Don't swear, Teddy! He isn't old, nor anything bad, but good and kind, and the best friend I've got, next to you. Don't fly into a passion. I haven't the least idea of loving him or anybody else."

"But you will after a while, and then what will become of me?"

"You'll love someone else too, like a sensible boy, and forget all this trouble."

"I *can't* love anyone else, and I'll never forget you, Jo. Never! Never!"

"You haven't heard what I wanted to tell you. Sit down and listen, for I want to do right and make you happy," she said, hoping to soothe him with a little reason, which proved that she knew nothing about love.

Seeing a ray of hope in that last speech, Laurie threw himself down on the grass at her feet, leaned his arm on the lower step of the stile, and looked up at her with an expectant face. How could she say hard things to him while he watched her with eyes full of love and longing, and lashes still wet with the bitter drop or two her hardness of heart had wrung from him? She gently turned his head away, saying, as she stroked the wavy hair which had been allowed to grow for her sake, "I agree with Mother that you and I are not suited to each other, because our quick tempers and strong wills would probably make us miserable, if we were so foolish as to . . ." Jo paused a little over the last word, but Laurie uttered it with a rapturous expression.

"Marry. No, we shouldn't! If you loved me, Jo, I should be a perfect saint, for you could make me anything you like."

"No, I can't. I've tried it and failed, and I won't risk our happiness by such a serious experiment. Now do be reasonable, and take a sensible view of the case," implored Jo, almost at her wit's end.

"I won't be reasonable, I don't want to take what you call 'a sensible view.' It won't help me, and it only makes you harder. I don't believe you've got any heart."

"I wish I hadn't."

There was a little quiver in Jo's voice, and, thinking it a good omen, Laurie turned round, bringing all his persuasive powers to bear as he said, "Don't disappoint us, dear! Everyone expects it. Grandpa has set his heart upon it, your people like it, and I can't get on without you. Say you will, and let's be happy. Do, do!"

"I can't say yes truly, so I won't say it at all. You'll see that I'm right, by-and-by, and thank me for it," she began solemnly.

"I'll be hanged if I do!" And Laurie bounced up off the grass, burning with indignation at the bare idea.

"Yes, you will!" persisted Jo. "You'll get over this after a while, and find some lovely accomplished girl, who will adore you and make a fine wife for your fine house. I shouldn't. I'm homely and awkward and odd, and we should quarrel—we can't help it even now, you see—and I shouldn't like elegant society and you would, and everything would be horrid!"

"Anything more?" asked Laurie, finding it hard to listen.

"Nothing more, except that I don't believe I shall ever marry."

"I know better!" broke in Laurie. "You think so now, but there'll come a time when you'll love somebody tremendously, and live and die for him. I know you will, it's your way, and I shall have to stand by and see it." He would have seemed comical, if his face had not been so tragic.

"Yes, I will live and die for him, if he ever comes and makes me love him in spite of myself, and you must do the best you can!" cried Jo, losing patience. "I shall always be fond of you, very fond indeed, as a friend. But I'll never marry you, and the sooner you believe it the better for both of us—so now!"

That speech was like fire to gunpowder. Laurie looked at her a minute as if he did not know what to do with himself, then turned sharply away, saying in a desperate sort of tone, "You'll be sorry some day, Jo."

"Oh, where are you going?" she cried, for his face frightened her.

"To the devil!" was the consoling answer.

For a minute Jo's heart stood still, as he swung himself down the bank toward the river, but Laurie had no thought of a melodramatic plunge. Some blind instinct led him to fling hat and coat into his boat, and row away with all his might, making better time up the river than he had done in many a race.

Jo drew a long breath, then went slowly home, feeling as if she had murdered some innocent thing, and buried it under the leaves. "Now I must go and prepare Mr. Laurence to be very kind to my poor boy. I wish he'd love Beth, perhaps he may in time, but I begin to think I was mistaken about her. Oh dear! How can girls like to have lovers and refuse them. I think it's dreadful."

She went straight to Mr. Laurence, told the hard story bravely, and then broke down, crying so dismally that the kind old gentleman, though sorely disappointed, did not utter a reproach. He found it difficult to understand how any girl could help loving Laurie, and hoped she would change her mind, but he knew even better than Jo that love cannot be forced.

When Laurie came home his grandfather met him as if he knew nothing. But when they sat together in the twilight, the time they used to enjoy so much, it was hard work for the old man to ramble on as usual, and harder still for the young one to listen to praises of the last year's success, which to him now seemed love's labor lost. He bore it as long as he could, then went to his piano and began to play. The windows were open, and Jo, walking in the garden with Beth, for once understood music better than her sister, for he played the "Sonata Pathetique," and played it as he never did before.

"That's very fine, I dare say, but it's sad enough to make one cry. Give us something gayer, lad," said Mr. Laurence, whose kind old heart was full of sympathy.

Laurie dashed into a livelier strain, played stormily for several minutes, and would have got through bravely, if in a momentary lull Mrs. March's voice had not been heard calling, "Jo, dear, come in. I want you."

Just what Laurie longed to say, with a different meaning! As he listened, he lost his place, the music ended with a broken chord, and the musician sat silent in the dark.

"I can't stand this," muttered the old gentleman. Up he got, groped his way to the piano, laid a kind hand on either of the broad shoulders, and said gently, "I know, my boy, I know."

No answer for an instant, then Laurie asked sharply, "Who told you?"

"Jo herself."

"Then there's nothing more to say!" And he shook off his grandfather's hands with an impatient motion, for though grateful for the sympathy, his man's pride could not bear a man's pity.

"I want to say one thing," returned Mr. Laurence with unusual mildness. "I'm disappointed, but the girl can't help it, and the only thing left for you to do is to go away for a time. Where will you go?"

"Anywhere. I don't care what becomes of me." And Laurie got up with a reckless laugh.

"Take it like a man, and don't do anything rash, for God's sake. Why not go abroad, as you planned, and forget it? You've been wild to go, and I promised you should when you got through college."

"Ah, but I didn't mean to go alone!" And Laurie walked fast through the room with an expression which it was well his grandfather did not see.

"I don't ask you to go alone. There's someone ready and glad to go with you, anywhere in the world."

"Who, sir?" stopping to listen.

"Myself."

Laurie came back as quickly as he went, and put out his hand, saying huskily, "I'm a selfish brute, but . . . you know . . . Grandfather . . ."

"Lord help me, yes, I do know, for I've been through it all before, once in my own young days, and then with your father. Now just sit quietly down and hear my plan. It's all settled, and can be carried out at once," said Mr. Laurence, keeping hold of the young man, as if fearful that he would break away as his father had done before him.

"Well, sir, what is it?" And Laurie sat down, without a sign of interest in face or voice.

"There is business in London that needs looking after. I meant you should attend to it, but I can do it better myself, and things here will get on well with Brooke to manage them. My partners do almost everything, I'm merely holding on till you take my place, and can be off at any time."

"But you hate traveling, sir. I can't ask it of you at your age," began Laurie, who was grateful for the sacrifice, but much preferred to go alone, if he went at all.

The old gentleman knew that perfectly well, but the mood in which he found his grandson assured him that it would not be wise. So, stifling a natural regret at the thought of the home comforts he would leave behind him, he said stoutly, "Bless your soul, I quite enjoy the idea. It will do me good, and my old bones won't suffer, for traveling nowadays is almost as easy as sitting in a chair."

A restless movement from Laurie suggested that he did not like the plan, and made the old man add hastily, "I don't intend to gad about with you, but leave you free to go where you like, while I amuse myself in my own way. I've friends in London and Paris, and should like to visit them. Meantime you can go to Italy, Germany, Switzerland, where you will, and enjoy pictures, music, scenery, and adventures to your heart's content."

Now, Laurie felt that his heart was entirely broken and the world a howling wilderness, but at the sound of certain words which the old gentleman artfully introduced into his closing sentence, the broken heart gave an unexpected leap, and a green oasis or two suddenly appeared in the howling wilderness. He sighed, and then said, in a spiritless tone, "Just as you like, sir. It doesn't matter where I go or what I do."

"It does to me, remember that, my lad. I give you entire liberty, but I trust you to make an honest use of it. Promise me that, Laurie."

"Anything you like, sir."

"Good," thought the old gentleman. "You don't care now, but there'll come a time when that promise will keep you out of mischief, or I'm much mistaken."

During the time necessary for preparation, Laurie bore himself as young gentlemen usually do in such cases. He was moody, irritable, and pensive by turns; lost his appetite, neglected his dress, and devoted much time to playing tempestuously on his piano. He avoided Jo, but consoled himself by staring at her from his window with a tragic face. Everyone rejoiced that the "poor, dear fellow was going away to forget his trouble, and come home happy." Of course, he smiled darkly at their delusion, but passed it by with the sad superiority of one who knew that his fidelity like his love was unchangeable.

When the parting came his gaiety did not deceive anybody, but they tried to look as if it did, and he got on well till Mrs. March kissed him. Then he hastily embraced them all round, not forgetting Hannah, and ran downstairs as if for his life. Jo followed a minute after to wave her hand to him if he looked round. He did look round, came back, put his arms about her as she stood on the step above him, and looked up at her with a face that made his short appeal both eloquent and pathetic.

"Oh, Jo, can't you?"

"Teddy, dear, I wish I could!"

That was all, except a little pause. Then Laurie straightened himself up, said, "It's all right, never mind," and went away without another word. Ah, but it wasn't all right, and Jo did mind. For while the curly head lay on her arm a minute after her hard answer, she felt as if she had stabbed her dearest friend, and when he left her without a look behind him, she knew that the boy Laurie never would come again.

13
BETH'S SECRET

WHEN JO CAME HOME THAT SPRING, she had been struck with the change in Beth. It had come too gradually to startle those who saw her daily, but to eyes sharpened by absence, it was very plain and a heavy weight fell on Jo's heart as she saw her sister's face. It was no paler and not much thinner than in the autumn, yet there was a strange, transparent look about it, as if the immortal was shining through the frail flesh with an indescribably pathetic beauty. Jo saw and felt it, but Beth seemed happy, no one appeared to doubt that she was better, and so Jo for a time forgot her fear.

But when Laurie was gone and peace prevailed again, the vague anxiety returned and haunted her. When she showed her savings and proposed the mountain trip, Beth had thanked her heartily, but begged not to go so far away from home. Another little visit to the seashore would suit her better, so Jo took Beth down to the quiet place, where she could let the fresh sea breezes blow a little color into her pale cheeks.

Among the pleasant people there, the girls made few friends, preferring to live for one another. They came and went, unaware of the interest they created in those about them, who watched with sympathetic eyes the strong sister and the feeble one, always together, as if they felt instinctively that a long separation was not far away.

Jo took Beth down to the quiet place, where she could let the fresh sea breezes blow a little color into her pale cheeks.

They did feel it, yet neither spoke of it, for often between ourselves and those nearest and dearest to us there exists a reserve which is hard to overcome. Jo wondered if her sister guessed the hard truth, and what thoughts were passing through her mind during the long hours when she lay on the warm rocks with her head in Jo's lap, while the winds blew healthfully over her and the sea made music at her feet.

One day Beth told her. Jo thought she was asleep, she lay so still, and putting down her book, sat looking at her with wistful eyes, trying to see signs of hope in the faint color on Beth's cheeks. But she could not find enough to satisfy her, for the cheeks were thin, and the hands seemed too feeble to hold even the rosy little shells they had been gathering. It came to her then more bitterly than ever that Beth was slowly drifting away from her, and her arms instinctively tightened their hold upon the dearest treasure she possessed. For a minute her eyes were too dim for seeing, and, when they cleared, Beth was looking up at her so tenderly that there was hardly any need for her to say, "Jo, dear, I'm glad you know it. I've tried to tell you, but I couldn't."

There was no answer except her sister's cheek against her own, not even tears, for when most deeply moved, Jo did not cry.

"I've known it for a good while, dear, and, now I'm used to it, it isn't hard to think of or to bear. Don't be troubled about me, because it's best. Indeed it is."

"Is this what made you so unhappy in the autumn, Beth?"

"Yes, I gave up hoping then, but I didn't like to admit it. I tried to think it was my imagination. But when I saw you all so well and strong and full of happy plans, it was hard to feel that I could never be like you, and then I was miserable, Jo."

"Oh, Beth, and you didn't tell me! How could you shut me out, and bear it all alone?"

Jo's heart ached to think of the solitary struggle that must have gone on while Beth learned to say goodbye to health, love, and life, and take up her cross so cheerfully.

"Perhaps it was wrong, but I tried to do right. No one said anything, and I hoped I was mistaken. It would have been selfish to frighten you all when Marmee was so anxious about Meg, and Amy away, and you so happy with Laurie—at least, I thought so then."

"And I thought that you loved him, Beth, and I went away because I couldn't," cried Jo, glad to say all the truth.

"Why, Jo, how could I, when he was so fond of you?" asked Beth, as innocently as a child. "I do love him dearly—he is so good to me! But he never could be anything to me but my brother. I hope he truly will be, sometime."

"Not through me," said Jo decidedly. "Amy is left for him, and they would suit excellently, but I have no heart for such things now. I don't care what becomes of anybody but you, Beth. You must get well."

"I want to, oh, so much! I try, but every day I lose a little, and feel more sure that I shall never gain it back. It's like the tide, Jo, when it turns, it goes slowly, but it can't be stopped."

"It shall be stopped, nineteen is too young. Beth, I can't let you go. I'll work and pray and fight against it. God won't be so cruel as to take you from me," cried poor Jo.

Simple, sincere people seldom speak much of their piety. It shows itself in acts rather than in words. Beth did not rebuke Jo with saintly speeches, only loved her better for her passionate affection, and clung more closely to the dear human love, through which our Father draws us closer to Himself. She could not say, "I'm glad to go," for life was sweet to her. She could only sob out, "I try to be willing," while she held fast to Jo, as the first bitter wave of this great sorrow broke over them together.

By-and-by Beth said, with recovered serenity, "You'll tell them this when we go home?"

"I think they will see it without words," sighed Jo, for now it seemed to her that Beth changed every day.

"Perhaps not. I've heard that the people who love best are often blindest to such things. If they don't see it, you will tell them for me. I don't want any secrets, and it's kinder to prepare them. Meg has John and the babies to comfort her, but you must stand by Father and Mother, won't you, Jo?"

"If I can. But, Beth, I don't give up yet," said Jo, trying to speak cheerfully.

Beth lay a minute thinking, and then said in her quiet way, "I have a feeling that it never was intended I should live long. I'm not like the rest of you. I never made any plans about what I'd do when I grew up. I never thought of being married, as you all did. I couldn't seem to imagine myself anything but stupid little Beth, trotting about at home, of no use anywhere but there. I never wanted to go away, and the hard part now is the leaving you all. I'm not afraid, but I might be homesick for you even in heaven."

Jo could not speak, and for several minutes there was no sound but the sigh of the wind and the lapping of the tide. A white-winged gull flew by, with the flash of sunshine on its silvery breast. Beth watched it till it vanished, and her eyes were full of sadness. A little gray-coated sand bird came tripping over the beach, "peeping" softly to itself, as if enjoying the sun and sea. It came close to Beth, looked at her with a friendly eye, and sat upon a warm stone, dressing its wet feathers, quite at home. Beth smiled and felt comforted, for the tiny thing seemed to offer its small friendship and remind her that a pleasant world was still to be enjoyed.

"Dear little bird! See, Jo, how tame it is. I used to call them my birds last summer, and Mother said they reminded her of me—busy, quaker-colored creatures, always near the shore, and always chirping that contented little song of theirs. You are the gull, Jo, strong and wild, fond of the storm and the wind, flying far out to sea, and happy all alone. Meg is the turtledove, and Amy is like the lark she writes about, trying to get up among the clouds, but always dropping down into its nest again. She's so ambitious, but her heart is good and tender, and no matter how high she flies, she never will forget home. I hope I shall see her again, but she seems so far away."

"She is coming in the spring, and I mean that you shall be all ready to see and enjoy her. I'm going to have you well and rosy by that time," began Jo.

"Jo, dear, don't hope any more. It won't do any good, I'm sure of that. We won't be miserable, but enjoy being together while we wait. We'll have happy times, for I don't suffer much, and I think the tide will go out easily, if you help me."

Jo leaned down to kiss the tranquil face, and with that silent kiss, she dedicated herself soul and body to Beth.

She was right—there was no need of any words when they got home, for Father and Mother saw plainly now. Tired with her short journey, Beth went at once to bed, saying how glad she was to be home, and when Jo went down, she found that she would be spared the hard task of telling Beth's secret. Her father stood leaning his head on the mantelpiece, and did not turn as she came in, but her mother stretched out her arms as if for help, and Jo went to comfort her without a word.

14
NEW IMPRESSIONS

AT THREE IN THE AFTERNOON, all the fashionable world at Nice, France, may be seen on the English Promenade. It is a wide walk bordered by palms, flowers, and tropical shrubs, bounded on one side by the sea, on the other by the grand drive, lined with hotels and villas, while beyond lie orange orchards and the hills. On a sunny day the spectacle is as gay and brilliant as a carnival. Visitors from many countries all drive, sit, or saunter here, chatting over the news, and criticizing the latest celebrity who has arrived.

Along this walk, on Christmas Day, a tall young man walked slowly, with his hands behind him. He looked like an Italian, was dressed like an Englishman, and had the independent air of an American—a combination which caused feminine eyes to look approvingly after him, and caused several dandies in black velvet suits, with rose-colored neckties, buff gloves, and orange flowers in their buttonholes, to shrug their shoulders and envy him his inches. The young man took little notice, except to glance now and then at some blonde girl or lady in blue.

Presently he strolled out of the promenade and stood a moment at the crossing. The quick trot of ponies' feet made him look up as one of the little carriages, containing a single lady, came rapidly down the street. The lady was young, blonde, and dressed in blue. He stared a minute, then his whole face woke up, and waving his hat like a boy, he hurried forward to meet her.

"Oh, Laurie, is it really you? I thought you'd never come!" cried Amy, dropping the reins and holding out both hands.

"I promised to spend Christmas with you, and here I am."

"How is your grandfather? When did you come? Where are you staying?"

"Very well—last night—at the Chauvain Hotel. I called at your hotel, but you were all out."

"I have so much to say, I don't know where to begin! Get in and we can talk at our ease. I was going for a drive and longing for company. There's a Christmas party tonight at our hotel. You'll go with us, of course? Aunt will be charmed."

"Thank you. Where now?" asked Laurie, leaning back and folding his arms. Amy went on driving, enjoying her dainty whip and the blue reins over the white ponies' backs.

"I'm going to the bankers first for letters, and then to Castle Hill. The view is so lovely, and I like to feed the peacocks. Have you ever been there?"

"Often, years ago, but I don't mind having a look at it."

"Now tell me all about yourself. The last I heard of you, your grandfather wrote that he expected you from Berlin."

"Yes, I spent a month there and then joined him in Paris, where he has settled for the winter. He has friends there and finds plenty to amuse him. He hates to travel, and I hate to keep still, so we each suit ourselves, and there is no trouble. I am often with him, and he enjoys my adventures, while I like to feel that someone is glad to see me when I get back from my wanderings. Dirty old hole, isn't it?" he added, with a look of disgust as they drove along the boulevard to the Place Napoleon in the old city.

"The dirt is picturesque, so I don't mind. The river and the hills are delicious, and these glimpses of the narrow cross streets are my delight. Now we shall have to wait for that procession to pass. It's going to the Church of St. John."

While Laurie listlessly watched the procession of priests and nuns, Amy watched him and felt a new sort of shyness steal over her, for he was changed, and she could not find the merry-faced boy she left in the moody-looking man beside her. He was handsomer than ever and greatly improved, she thought, but now that the flush of pleasure at meeting her was over, he looked tired and spiritless—not sick, nor exactly unhappy, but older and graver. She couldn't understand it and did not venture to ask questions.

"*Que pensez-vous?*" she said, airing her French, which had improved in quantity, if not in quality, since she came abroad.

"That mademoiselle has made good use of her time, and the result is charming," replied Laurie, bowing, with his hand on his heart and an admiring look.

She blushed with pleasure, but somehow the compliment did not satisfy her as much as when he used to tell her she was "altogether jolly," with a hearty smile and an approving pat on the head. He seemed less sincere now.

"If that's the way he's going to grow up, I wish he'd stay a boy," she thought, trying to seem happy and at ease.

At Avigdor's she found the letters from home and, giving the reins to Laurie, read them luxuriously as they wound up the shady road between green hedges, where tea roses bloomed as freshly as in June.

"Beth is very poorly, Mother says. I often think I ought to go home, but they all say, 'stay.' So I do, for I shall never have another chance like this," said Amy, looking sober over one page.

"I think you are right, there. You could do nothing at home, and it is a great comfort to them to know that you are well and happy, and enjoying so much, my dear."

He drew a little nearer, and looked more like his old self as he said that. The brotherly "my dear" seemed to assure her that if any trouble did come, she would not be alone in a strange land. Presently she laughed and showed him a small sketch of Jo in her scribbling suit and issuing from her mouth the words, "Genius burns!"

Laurie smiled, took it, put it in his vest pocket "to keep it from blowing away," and listened with interest to the lively letter Amy read him.

"This will be a regularly merry Christmas to me, with presents in the morning, you and letters in the afternoon, and a party at night," said Amy, as they alighted among the ruins of the old fort, and a flock of splendid peacocks came trooping about them. While Amy stood laughing on the bank above him as she scattered crumbs to the brilliant birds, Laurie looked at her as she had looked at him, with a natural curiosity. She was as sprightly and graceful as ever, with the addition of that indescribable something we call elegance—a bright-faced girl standing in the sunshine, which brought out the soft hue of her dress, the fresh color of her cheeks, the golden gloss of her hair.

As they came up onto the stone plateau that crowns the hill, Amy waved her hand as if welcoming him to her favorite haunt, and said, pointing here and there, "Do you remember the Cathedral and the Corso, the fishermen dragging their nets in the bay, and the lovely road to Villa Franca, Schubert's Tower, just below, and, best of all, that speck far out to sea which they say is Corsica?"

"I remember, it's not much changed," he answered, without enthusiasm.

"What Jo would give for a sight of that famous speck!" said Amy, feeling in good spirits and anxious to see him so also. "Take a good look at it for her sake, and then come and tell me what you have been doing with yourself all this while."

Though Laurie was polite and answered all her questions freely, he was listless. After idling away an hour, he drove back to her hotel with her, promising to return in the evening.

Amy deliberately primped that night. She had seen her old friend in a new light, not as "our boy" but as a handsome and agreeable man. Amy knew her good points, and made the most of them with the taste and skill which is a fortune to a poor and pretty woman.

"I do want him to think I look well, and tell them so at home," said Amy to herself, as she put on Flo's old white silk ball dress, and covered it with a cloud of fresh illusion, out of which her white shoulders and golden head emerged with a most artistic effect. Her hair she had the sense to leave alone, after gathering up the thick waves and curls into a knot at the back of her head.

"It's not the fashion, but it's becoming, and I can't afford to make a fright of myself," she used to say, when advised to frizzle, puff, or braid, as the latest style commanded.

Amy looped her snowy skirts with rosy clusters of azalea, and framed the white shoulders in delicate green vines. Remembering the old painted boots, she surveyed her white satin slippers with girlish satisfaction.

She glided down to the lobby and walked up and down the long hall while waiting for Laurie. Once she lingered under the chandelier, which had a good effect upon her hair, then went away to the other end of the room, as if ashamed of the desire to impress him. It so happened that she could not have done a better thing, for Laurie came in so quietly she did not hear him, and as she stood at the distant window, with her head half turned and one hand gathering up her dress, the slender, white figure against the red curtains was as effective as a well-placed statue.

They greeted each other. "Here are your flowers. I arranged them myself," said Laurie, handing her a delicate nosegay held in a silver bracelet she had long admired in a jeweler's window. "It isn't all it should be, but your beauty has improved it," he added, as she snapped the silver bracelet on her wrist.

"Please don't talk that way."

"I thought you liked that sort of thing."

"Not from you. It doesn't sound natural, and I like your old plain talk better."

"I'm glad of it," he answered, with a look of relief, then buttoned her gloves for her and asked if his tie was straight, just as he used to do when they went to parties together at home.

The company assembled that evening was such as one sees nowhere but on the Continent. The hospitable Americans had invited every acquaintance they had in Nice, and having no prejudice against titles, secured a few members of European nobility to add luster to their Christmas ball.

Any young girl can imagine Amy's state of mind when she "took the stage" that night, leaning on Laurie's arm. With the first burst of the band, Amy's color rose, her eyes began to sparkle, and her feet to tap the floor impatiently, for she danced well and wanted Laurie to know it. Therefore the shock she received can better be imagined than described, when he said in a perfectly tranquil tone, "Do you care to dance?"

"One usually does at a ball."

"I meant the first dance. May I have the honor?"

"I can give you one if I put off the Count. He dances divinely, but he will excuse me, as you are an old friend," said Amy, hoping to show Laurie that she was not to be trifled with.

After the initial dance, Laurie handed her over to the Count without reserving any future dances in her ball book, which was soon full of names until supper. When he asked for another dance he was too late, and as she danced away with the Count, she saw Laurie sit down by her aunt with an actual expression of relief.

That was unpardonable, and Amy took no more notice of him for a long while, except a word now and then when she came to her aunt between the dances for a necessary pin or a moment's rest. Her anger had a good effect, however, for she hid it under a smiling face, and seemed unusually blithe and brilliant. Laurie's eyes followed her with pleasure, for she danced with spirit and grace.

Soon the spirit of the season took possession of everyone, and Christmas merriment made all faces shine, hearts happy, and heels light. The musicians fiddled, tooted, and banged as if they enjoyed it, everybody danced who could, and those who couldn't admired their neighbors with uncommon warmth.

Amy and the Count distinguished themselves with their enthusiasm and graceful agility, and Laurie found himself involuntarily keeping time to the rhythmic rise and fall of her white slippers that flew by as if winged. At last she was ready to rest, and see how her naughty knight had borne his punishment.

It had been successful, for Laurie had a waked-up look as he rose to give her his seat. And when he hurried away to bring her some supper, she said to herself, with a satisfied smile, "Ah, I thought that would do him good!"

"You look like a painted woman," he said, as he fanned her with one hand and held her coffee cup in the other.

"My rouge won't come off." And Amy rubbed her brilliant cheek, and showed him her white glove with a sober simplicity that made him laugh outright.

"What do you call this stuff?" he asked, touching a fold of her dress that had blown over his knee.

"Illusion."

"Good name for it. It's pretty—something new, isn't it?"

"It's as old as the hills. You've seen it on dozens of girls, and you never found out that it was pretty till now, silly."

"I never saw it on you before, which accounts for the mistake, you see."

"None of that. I'd rather take coffee than compliments just now. No, don't lounge, it makes me nervous."

Laurie sat bolt upright and meekly took her empty plate, feeling an odd sort of pleasure in having "little Amy" order him about, for she had lost her shyness now, as girls have a delightful way of doing when lords of creation show any signs of subjection.

"Where did you learn all this sort of thing?" he asked with a quizzical look.

Amy was gratified, but of course didn't show it, and demurely answered, "Foreign life polishes one in spite of one's self. And as for this"—with a little gesture toward her dress—"why, I am used to making the most of my poor little things."

Amy regretted that last sentence, fearing it wasn't in good taste. But Laurie liked her the better for it, and found himself both admiring and respecting the brave patience that made the most of opportunity, and the cheerful spirit that covered poverty with flowers.

15
ON THE SHELF

As she was a womanly little woman, Meg was entirely absorbed in her children, to the utter exclusion of everything and everybody else. Day and night she brooded over them with tireless devotion and anxiety, leaving John to the tender mercies of the hired help, for an Irish lady now presided over the kitchen department. As he adored his babies, he cheerfully relinquished his comfort for a time, supposing with masculine ignorance that peace would soon be restored. But three months passed, and there was no return of repose. Meg looked worn and nervous, the babies absorbed every minute of her time, the house was neglected, and Kitty, the cook, who took life easy, didn't feed him well.

When he came in at night, eager to embrace his family, he was quenched by, "Hush! They are just asleep after worrying all day." If he proposed a little amusement at home, "No, it would disturb the babies." If he hinted at a lecture or concert, he was answered with a reproachful look, and a firm, "Leave my children for pleasure? Never!" His sleep was broken by infant wails; his meals were interrupted if a muffled chirp sounded from the nest above; and when he read his paper in the evening, Mrs. Brooke was only interested in her household news.

Home was merely a nursery, and the perpetual "hushing" made him feel like a brutal intruder whenever he entered the sacred precincts of Babyland. He bore it patiently for six months, and, when no signs of improvement appeared, he did what other paternal exiles do— tried to get a little comfort elsewhere. Scott had married and lived not far off, and John fell into the way of running over for an hour or two in an evening, when his own wife was singing lullabies that seemed to have no end. Mrs. Scott was a lively, pretty girl, with nothing to do but be agreeable. The parlor was always bright and attractive, the chess- board ready, the piano in tune, plenty of gossip, and a nice little sup- per set forth in tempting style.

John would have preferred his own fireside if it had not been so lonely, but he gratefully took the next best thing and enjoyed his neighbor's companionship.

Meg approved of the new arrangement at first, and found it a relief to know that John was having a good time. But by-and-by, when the teething worry was over and the idols went to sleep at proper hours, leaving Mamma time to rest, she began to miss John. She felt injured because he did not know that she wanted him without being told, entirely forgetting the many evenings he had waited for her in vain. Lack of exercise robs young mothers of cheerfulness, and too much devotion to that idol of American women, the teapot, makes them feel as if they were all nerve and no muscle.

"Yes," she would say, looking in the glass, "I'm getting old and ugly. John doesn't find me interesting any longer, so he leaves his faded wife and goes to see his pretty neighbor. Well, the babies love me, they don't care if I am thin and pale and haven't time to crimp my hair. They are my comfort, and some day John will see what I've gladly sac- rificed for them, won't he, my precious?"

To which pathetic appeal Daisy would answer with a coo or Demi with a gurgle, which soothed Meg for the time being. But the pain increased as politics absorbed John, who was always running over to discuss interesting points with Scott, unaware that Meg missed him.

Her mother found her in tears one day, and insisted on knowing what the matter was.

"I wouldn't tell anyone except you, Mother, but I do need advice, for if John goes on so much longer I might as well be widowed."

"Goes on how, my dear?" asked her mother anxiously.

"He's away all day, and at night, when I want to see him, he is continually going over to the Scotts'. It isn't fair that I should have the hardest work, and never any amusement. Men are selfish, even the best of them."

"So are women. Don't blame John till you see where you are wrong yourself. Did John ever neglect you, as you call it, while you made it a point to give him your company in the evening, his only leisure time?"

"No, but I can't do it now, with two babies to tend."

"I think you could, dear, and I think you ought. May I speak freely?"

Meg drew her low chair beside her mother's, and the two women rocked and talked.

"You have only made the mistake that most young wives make—forgotten your duty to your husband in your love for your children. A natural and forgivable mistake, Meg, but children should draw you nearer than ever, not separate you, as if they were all yours, and John had nothing to do but support them. Besides, you owe something to John as well as to the babies. Don't neglect husband for children, don't shut him out of the nursery, but teach him how to help in it. His place is there as well as yours, and the children need him."

"You really think so, Mother?"

"I know it, Meg. When you and Jo were little, I went on just as you are, feeling as if I didn't do my duty unless I devoted myself wholly to you. Poor Father took to his books, after I had refused all offers of help, and left me to try my experiment alone. I struggled along as well as I could, but Jo was too much for me. I nearly spoiled her by indulgence. You were poorly, and I worried about you till I fell sick myself. Then Father came to the rescue, quietly managed everything, and made himself so helpful that I saw my mistake, and never have been able to get on without him since. That is the secret of our home happiness—he does not let business wean him from the little cares and duties of the home, and I try not to let domestic worries destroy my interest in his pursuits."

"John is so sensible, I'm afraid he will think I'm stupid if I ask questions about politics and things."

"I don't believe he would. Love covers a multitude of sins. Try it, and see if he doesn't find your society far more agreeable than Mrs. Scott's suppers."

"I will. Poor John! I'm afraid I have neglected him sadly, but I thought I was right, and he never said anything."

"This is just the time, Meg, when young married people are apt to grow apart, and the very time when they ought to be most together. For the first tenderness soon wears off, unless care is taken to preserve it, and no time is so beautiful and precious to parents as the first years of the little lives given them to train. Don't let John be a stranger to the babies, for they will do more to keep him safe and happy in this world of trial and temptation than anything else."

A few days after the talk with her mother, Meg resolved to try a social evening with John. She ordered a nice supper, set the parlor in order, dressed herself pretty, and put the children to bed early, that nothing should interfere with her experiment. But unfortunately Demi's most unconquerable prejudice was against going to bed, and that night he decided to go on a rampage. Poor Meg sang and rocked, told stories and tried every sleep-provoking wile she could devise, but all in vain—the big eyes wouldn't shut. Long after Daisy had gone to sleep, like the chubby little bunch of good nature she was, Demi lay staring at the light, wide-awake.

"Will Demi lie still like a good boy, while Mamma runs down and gives poor Papa his tea?" asked Meg, as the hall door softly closed, and the well-known step went tip-toeing into the dining room.

"Me has tea!" said Demi, preparing to join the party.

"No, but I'll save you some little cakies for breakfast, if you'll go bye-bye like Daisy. Will you?"

"Iss!" and Demi shut his eyes tight, as if to catch sleep and hurry the desired day.

Taking advantage of the moment, Meg slipped away and ran down to greet her husband with a smiling face and the little blue bow in her hair which was his special admiration. He saw it at once and said with pleased surprise, "Why, little mother, how nice you look tonight. Do you expect company?"

"Only you, dear."

"Is it a birthday, anniversary, or anything?"

"No, I'm tired of being a dowdy, so I dressed up for a change. You always make yourself nice for dinner, no matter how tired you are, so why shouldn't I when I have the time?"

"I do it out of respect to you, my dear," said old-fashioned John.

"Ditto, ditto, Mr. Brooke," laughed Meg, looking young and pretty again, as she nodded to him over the teapot.

"Well, it's altogether delightful, and like old times." And John sipped his tea with an air of rapture, which was of short duration however, for as he put down his cup, the door handle rattled mysteriously, and a little voice was heard, saying impatiently, "Opy doy. Me's tummin!"

"It's that naughty boy. I told him to go to sleep, and here he is, downstairs, getting his death a-cold," said Meg, opening the door.

"Mornin' now," announced Demi in a joyful tone as he entered, with his long nightgown gracefully festooned over his arm and every curl bobbing gaily as he pranced about the table, eying the "cakies" with loving glances.

"No, it isn't morning yet. You must go to bed, and not trouble poor Mamma. Then you can have the little cake with sugar on it."

"Me loves Parpar," said the artful one, preparing to climb his father's knee and revel in forbidden joys. But John shook his head, and said to Meg, "If you told him to stay up there, and go to sleep alone, make him do it, or he will never learn to mind you."

"Yes, of course. Come, Demi." And Meg led her son away, feeling a strong desire to spank him. He hopped beside her, expecting a bribe as soon as they reached the nursery.

Nor was he disappointed, for that shortsighted woman actually gave him a lump of sugar, tucked him into his bed, and forbade any more visits until morning.

"Iss!" said Demi, blissfully sucking his sugar, and regarding his first attempt as eminently successful.

Meg returned to her place, and supper was progressing pleasantly, when the little ghost walked in again and boldly demanded, "More sudar, Marmar."

"Now this won't do," said John, hardening his heart against the engaging little sinner. "We shall never know any peace till that child learns to go to bed properly. You have made a slave of yourself long enough. Give him one lesson, and then there will be an end of it. Put him in his bed and leave him, Meg."

"He won't stay there. He never does unless I sit by him."

"I'll manage him. Demi, go upstairs, and get into your bed, as Mamma bids you."

"Shant!" replied the young rebel, helping himself to the coveted "cakie," and beginning to eat it with calm audacity.

"You must never say that to Papa. I shall carry you if you don't go yourself."

"Go 'way, me don't love Parpar." And Demi retired to his mother's skirts for protection.

But even that refuge proved unavailing, for he was delivered over to his father with a "Be gentle with him, John," which struck the culprit with dismay, for when Mamma deserted him, then the judgment day was at hand. Demi could not restrain his wrath, but openly defied

Papa, and kicked and screamed all the way upstairs. The minute he was put into bed on one side, he rolled out on the other, and made for the door, only to be caught up and put back again. This lively performance was kept up till the young man's strength gave out, when he devoted himself to roaring at the top of his voice. John sat as unmoved as the post which is popularly believed to be deaf. No coaxing, no sugar, no lullaby, no story. This new order of things disgusted him, and he howled dismally for "Marmar." The plaintive wail which followed the passionate roar went to Meg's heart, and she ran up to say beseechingly, "Let me stay with him, or he will cry himself sick, John."

"No, he won't. He's so tired he will soon drop off and then the matter is settled, for he will understand that he has to mind. Don't interfere, I'll manage him."

"He's my child, and I can't have his spirit broken by harshness."

"He's my child, and I won't have his temper spoiled by indulgence. Go down, my dear, and leave the boy to me."

"Please let me kiss him once, John?"

"Certainly. Demi, say good night to Mamma, and let her go and rest, for she is tired with taking care of you all day."

Meg always insisted upon it that the kiss won the victory, for after it was given, Demi sobbed more quietly and lay still at the bottom of the bed, whither he had wriggled in his anguish of mind.

"Poor little man, he's worn out with sleep and crying. I'll cover him up, and then go and set Meg's heart at rest," thought John, creeping to the bedside, hoping to find his rebellious heir asleep.

But he wasn't, for the moment his father peeped at him, Demi's eyes opened, his little chin began to quiver, and he put up his arms, saying, "Me's dood, now."

Sitting on the stairs outside, imagining all sorts of impossible accidents, Meg slipped into the room to set her fears at rest. Demi lay fast asleep, not in his usual spread-eagle attitude, but in a subdued bunch, cuddled close in the circle of his father's arm and holding his father's finger, as if he had gone to sleep a sadder and a wiser baby. John had waited till the little hand relaxed its hold, and while waiting had fallen asleep, more tired by that tussle with his son than with his whole day's work.

As Meg stood watching the two faces on the pillow, she smiled to herself, and then slipped away again, saying in a satisfied tone, "I never need fear that John will be too harsh with my babies. He will be a great help, for Demi is getting too much for me."

When John came down at last, expecting to find a reproachful wife, he was agreeably surprised to find Meg placidly trimming a bonnet, and to be greeted with the request to read something about the election, if he was not too tired. John saw in a minute that a revolution of some kind was going on, but wisely asked no questions. He read a long debate and then explained it in his most lucid manner, while Meg tried to look deeply interested, to ask intelligent questions, and keep her thoughts from wandering from the state of the nation to the state of her bonnet. In her secret soul, however, she decided that politics were as bad as mathematics. But she kept this idea to herself, and when John paused, shook her head and said with what she thought diplomatic ambiguity, "Well, I don't see what we are coming to."

John laughed, and watched her for a minute, as she poised a pretty little preparation of lace and flowers on her hand, and regarded it with the genuine interest which his lecture had failed to waken.

"She is trying to like politics for my sake, so I'll try and like millinery for hers, that's only fair," thought John the Just, adding aloud, "That's pretty. Is it what you call a breakfast cap?"

"My dear man, it's a bonnet! My best go-to-concert-and-theater bonnet."

"I beg your pardon, it was so small. How do you keep it on?"

"These bits of lace are fastened under the chin with a rosebud, so." And Meg illustrated by putting on the bonnet and regarding him with an air of calm satisfaction that was irresistible.

"It's a lovely bonnet, but I prefer the face inside, for it looks young and happy again." And John kissed the smiling face, to the great detriment of the rosebud under the chin.

"I'm glad you like it, for I want you to take me to one of the new concerts some night. I need some music to put me in tune. Will you, please?"

"Of course I will, with all my heart, or anywhere else you like. You have been shut up so long, it will do you no end of good, and I shall enjoy it. What put it into your head, little mother?"

"Well, I had a talk with Marmee the other day, and she said I needed change and less care. So Hannah is to help me with the children, and I'm to see things about the house more, and now and then have a little fun. It's only an experiment, John, and I want to try it for your sake as much as for mine, because I've neglected you shamefully lately, and I'm going to make home what it used to be, if I can."

Never mind what John said, or what a narrow escape the little bonnet had from utter ruin. All that we have any business to know is that John did not appear to object. It was not all Paradise after that by any means, but everyone was better. Accurate, steadfast John brought order and obedience into Babydom, while Meg recovered her spirits with plenty of exercise, a little pleasure, and much conversation with her sensible husband. Home grew homelike again.

The Scotts came to the Brookes' now, and everyone found the little house a cheerful place, full of happiness and family love. Even Sallie Moffat liked to go there. "It is always so quiet and pleasant here, it does me good, Meg," she used to say, looking about her with wistful eyes, as if trying to discover the charm, that she might use it in her great house, full of splendid loneliness. There were no sunny-faced babies there, and Ned lived in a world of his own, where there was no place for her.

This household happiness did not come all at once, but John and

Meg had found the key to it, and each year of married life taught them how to use it, unlocking the treasuries of real home love and mutual helpfulness, which the poorest may possess, and the richest cannot buy.

16
LAZY LAURENCE

LAURIE WENT TO NICE intending to stay a week, and remained a month. He and Amy were much together, riding, walking, dancing, or dawdling, for at Nice no one can be very industrious during the tourist season. They were half-consciously making discoveries and forming opinions about each other, and as Amy rose daily in the estimation of her friend, he sank in hers.

Laurie would have given Amy all the trinkets in Nice if she would have taken them, but at the same time he felt that he could not change the opinion she was forming of him, and he dreaded the keen blue eyes that seemed to watch him with such half-sorrowful, half-scornful surprise.

"I am going to Valrosa to sketch, will you come?" said Amy, as she joined Laurie one lovely day when he lounged in as usual about noon.

"Well, yes, but isn't it rather warm for such a long walk?" he answered slowly.

"I'm going to have the little carriage, and Baptiste can drive, so you'll have nothing to do but hold your umbrella, and keep your gloves nice," returned Amy, with a sarcastic glance at the immaculate kid gloves, which were a weak point with Laurie.

"Then I'll go with pleasure." He put out his hand to carry her

Laurie and Amy were much together, riding, walking, dancing, or dawdling.

144

sketchbook, but she tucked it under her arm with a sharp, "Don't trouble yourself. It's no exertion to me, but you don't look equal to it."

Laurie lifted his eyebrows and followed at a leisurely pace as she ran downstairs, but when they got into the carriage he took the reins himself, and left little Baptiste nothing to do but fold his arms and fall asleep on his perch.

The two never quarreled—Amy was too well-bred, and Laurie was too lazy—so in a minute he peeped under her hatbrim with an inquiring air. She answered with a smile, and they went on together in a most friendly manner.

It was a lovely drive. Here an ancient monastery. There a bare-legged shepherd in wooden shoes sat piping on a stone while his goats skipped among the rocks or lay at his feet. Brown, soft-eyed children ran out from the quaint stone hovels to offer bunches of oranges still on the bough. Gnarled olive trees covered the hills with their dusky foliage, fruit hung golden in the orchard, and great scarlet flowers fringed the roadside. Beyond, the Maritime Alps rose sharp and white against the blue Italian sky.

In that climate of perpetual summer roses blossomed everywhere. They overhung the archway and wound through lemon trees and feathery palms up to the villa on the hill. Every shadowy nook, where seats invited one to stop and rest, was a mass of bloom, every cool grotto had its marble nymph smiling from a veil of flowers, and every fountain reflected crimson, white, or pale pink roses. Roses covered the walls of the house, draped the cornices, climbed the pillars, and ran riot over the balustrade of the wide terrace, whence one looked down on the sunny Mediterranean, and the white-walled city on its shore.

"This is a regular honeymoon paradise, isn't it? Did you ever see such roses?" asked Amy, pausing on the terrace to enjoy the view, and a luxurious whiff of perfume that came wandering by.

"No, nor felt such thorns," returned Laurie, with his thumb in his mouth, after a vain attempt to reach a solitary scarlet flower, thinking of Jo as he did, for vivid flowers became her.

"Try lower down, and pick those that have no thorns," said Amy, gathering three of the tiny cream-colored ones from the wall behind her. She put them in his buttonhole as a peace offering.

"Laurie, when are you going to your grandfather?" she asked presently.

"Very soon."

"You have said that a dozen times within the last three weeks."

"I dare say, short answers save trouble."

"Then why don't you do it?"

"Natural depravity, I suppose."

"Natural indolence, you mean. It's really dreadful!" Amy looked severe.

Laurie stretched out on the broad ledge of the balustrade. Amy shook her head and opened her sketchbook with an air of resignation, but in a minute she began again.

"What are you doing with yourself?"

"Watching lizards."

"No, no. I mean what do you intend and wish to do?"

"Smoke a cigar, if you'll allow me."

"How provoking you are! I don't approve and I will only allow it on condition that you let me put you into my sketch."

"With all the pleasure in life. How will you have me—full-length or three-quarters, on my head or my heels?

"Stay as you are, and go to sleep if you like. I intend to work hard," said Amy in her most energetic tone.

"What delightful enthusiasm!" And he leaned against a tall urn with an air of entire satisfaction.

"What would Jo say if she saw you now?" asked Amy impatiently, hoping to stir him up by the mention of her energetic sister's name.

"As usual, 'Go away, Teddy, I'm busy!' " He laughed as he spoke, but

Amy looked up in time to catch a new expression on Laurie's face—a hard, bitter look, full of pain, dissatisfaction, and regret. It was gone before she could study it and the listless expression returned.

"You look like the effigy of a young knight asleep on his tomb," she said, carefully tracing his profile set off by the dark stone.

"Wish I was!"

"That's a foolish wish, unless you have spoiled your life. You are so changed, I sometimes think . . ." There Amy stopped, with a half-timid, half-wistful look, more significant than her unfinished speech.

Laurie saw and understood her affectionate anxiety, and looking straight into her eyes, said, just as he used to say it to her mother, "Everything's all right, ma'am."

"I'm glad of that!" she answered. "I didn't think you'd been a bad boy, but I fancied you might have been gambling or lost your heart to some charming Frenchwoman with a husband. Don't stay out there in the sun, come and lie on the grass here and let us share secrets."

Laurie obediently threw himself down on the lawn, and began to amuse himself by sticking daisies into the ribbons of Amy's hat, that lay there. "I'm all ready for the secrets." And he glanced up with interest.

"I've none to tell. You may begin."

"When do you begin your great work of art?" he asked.

"Never," she answered, with a despondent air. "Rome took all the vanity out of me, for after seeing the art wonders there, I gave up all my foolish hopes in despair."

"Why should you, with so much energy and talent?"

"That's just why—because talent isn't genius, and no amount of energy can make it so."

"And what are you going to do with yourself now, if I may ask?"

"Polish up my other talents, and be an ornament to society, if I get the chance."

Laurie smiled, but he liked the spirit with which she took up a new purpose when a long-cherished one died, and spent no time lamenting.

"Good! And here is where Fred Vaughn comes in, I fancy. Now I'm going to play brother, and ask questions. May I?"

"I don't promise to answer."

"Your face will, if your tongue won't. You aren't woman of the world enough yet to hide your feelings, my dear. I heard rumors about Fred and you last year, and it's my private opinion that if he had not been called home so suddenly and detained so long, something would have come of it."

"That's not for me to say," was Amy's prim reply, but her lips would smile, and there was a sparkle in her eye.

"You are not engaged, I hope?" And Laurie looked elder-brotherly and grave all of a sudden.

"No."

"But you will be, if he comes back and goes properly down upon his knees, won't you?"

"Very likely."

"He's a good fellow, Amy, but not the man I fancied you'd like."

"He is rich, a gentleman, and has delightful manners," began Amy, trying to be dignified, but feeling a little ashamed of herself.

"I understand. Queens of society can't get on without money, so you mean to make a good match. Quite right and proper, as the world goes, but it sounds odd from the lips of one of your mother's girls."

"True, nevertheless."

Laurie laid himself down again, with a sense of disappointment he could not explain. His silence, as well as her own self-disapproval, ruffled Amy, and made her resolve to deliver her lecture without delay.

"I wish you'd do me the favor to rouse yourself a little," she said sharply.

"Do it for me, there's a dear girl. I give you leave." Laurie enjoyed having someone to tease.

"You'd be angry in five minutes."

"It won't hurt me and it may amuse you, as the big man said when his little wife beat him. Regard me in the light of a husband or a carpet, and beat till you are tired, if that sort of exercise agrees with you."

Amy sharpened both tongue and pencil, and began, "Flo and I have a new name for you. It's 'Lazy Laurence.' How do you like it?"

She thought it would annoy him, but he only folded his arms under his head, with an imperturbable "That's not bad. Thank you, ladies."

"Do you want to know what I honestly think of you?"

"Pining to be told."

"Well, I despise you."

If she had even said "I hate you" in a petulant or coquettish tone, he would have laughed and rather liked it, but the grave, almost sad accent of her voice made him open his eyes, and ask quickly, "Why?"

"Because, with every chance for being good, useful, and happy, you are faulty, lazy, and miserable."

"Strong language, mademoiselle."

"If you like it, I'll go on."

"Pray, do. It's quite interesting."

"I thought you'd find it so. Selfish people always like to talk about themselves."

"Am I selfish?" The question slipped out involuntarily and in a tone of surprise, for the one virtue on which he prided himself was generosity.

"Yes, very," continued Amy, in a calm, cool voice. "Here you have been abroad nearly six months, and done nothing but waste time and money and disappoint your friends."

"Isn't a fellow to have any pleasure after a four-year grind?"

"You don't look as if you'd had much. At any rate, you are none the better for it, as far as I can see. You have grown abominably lazy. With money, talent, position, health, and beauty to use and enjoy, you can find nothing to do but dawdle, and instead of being the man you might and ought to be, you are only . . ." There she stopped, with a look that had both pain and pity in it.

The lecture began to take effect, for there was a wide-awake sparkle in Laurie's eyes now and a half-angry, half-injured expression replaced the former indifference. In a minute a hand came down over Amy's page, so that she could not draw, and Laurie's voice said, with a droll imitation of a penitent child, "I will be good, oh, I will be good!"

But Amy did not laugh, for she was in earnest, and tapping on the outspread hand with her pencil, said soberly, "Aren't you ashamed of a hand like that? It's as soft and white as a woman's, and looks as if it never did anything but wear expensive gloves and pick flowers for ladies. I'm glad to see there are no diamond rings on it, only the little old ring Jo gave you so long ago. Dear soul, I wish she was here to help me!"

"So do I!"

She glanced down at him with a new thought, but he was lying with his hat half over his face, as if for shade, and his mustache hid his mouth. She only saw his chest rise and fall, with a long breath that might have been a sigh, and the hand that wore the ring nestled down into the grass, as if to hide something. All in a minute Amy realized that Laurie never spoke voluntarily of Jo. She had fancied that perhaps a love trouble was at the bottom of the change in him, and now she was sure of it.

Her keen eyes filled, and when she spoke again, it was in a voice that could be beautifully soft and kind when she chose to make it so. "I know I have no right to talk so to you, Laurie, and if you weren't the sweetest-tempered fellow in the world, you'd be angry with me. But we are all so fond and proud of you, I couldn't bear to think they should be disappointed in you at home, though perhaps they would understand better than I do."

"I think they would," came from under the hat, in a grim tone.

"They ought to have told me, and not let me go blundering and scolding, when I should have been more kind and patient than ever. I never did like that Miss Randal and now I hate her!" Amy was clever, wishing to be sure of her facts this time.

"Hang Miss Randal!" And Laurie knocked the hat off his face with a look that left no doubt of his sentiments toward that young lady.

"I beg pardon, I thought . . ." And there she paused diplomatically.

"No, you didn't. You knew perfectly well I never cared for anyone but Jo." Laurie said that in his old, impetuous tone, and turned his face away as he spoke.

"I did think so, but as they never said anything about it, and you came away, I supposed I was mistaken. And Jo wouldn't be kind to you? Why, I was sure she loved you dearly."

"She was kind, but not in the right way. It's lucky for her she didn't love me, if I'm the good-for-nothing fellow you think me. It's her fault, though, and you may tell her so." The hard, bitter look came back again as he said that.

"I was wrong. I'm sorry I was so cross, but I can't help wishing you'd bear it better, Teddy, dear."

"Don't, that's her name for me!" Then as he pulled up grass by the handful, he added in a low voice, "Wait till you've tried it yourself."

"I'd take it bravely, if I couldn't be loved," said Amy, with the confidence of one who knew nothing about it.

Now, Laurie flattered himself that he had borne it remarkably well, asking no sympathy and taking his trouble away to live it down alone. Amy's lecture put the matter in a new light, and for the first time it did look weak and selfish to lose heart at the first failure, and shut himself up in moody indifference. Presently he sat up and asked slowly, "Do you think Jo would despise me as you do?"

"Yes, if she saw you now. She hates lazy people. Why don't you do something splendid, and make her love you?"

"I did my best, but it was no use."

"Graduating well, you mean? That was no more than you ought to have done, for your grandfather's sake. It did you good and proved that you could do something if you tried. If you'd only set about another task of some sort, you'd soon be your hearty, happy self again, and forget your trouble."

"That's impossible."

"Try it and see. You needn't shrug your shoulders and think, 'Much she knows about such things.' I'm interested in other people's experiences and inconsistencies, and I remember and use them for my own benefit. Love Jo all your days, if you choose, but don't let it spoil you, for it's wicked to throw away so many good gifts because you can't have the one you want. There, I won't lecture any more, for I know you'll wake up and be a man in spite of that hardhearted girl."

Neither spoke for several minutes. Laurie sat turning the little ring on his finger, and Amy put the last touches to the hasty sketch she had been working at while she talked. Presently she put it on his knee, merely saying, "How do you like that?"

He looked and then he smiled, as he could not well help doing, for it was well done—the long, lazy figure on the grass, with listless face, half-shut eyes, and one hand holding a cigar, from which came the little wreath of smoke that encircled the dreamer's head.

"How well you draw!" he said, with a genuine surprise and pleasure at her skill, adding, with a half-laugh, "Yes, that's me."

"As you are. This is as you were." And Amy laid another sketch beside the one he held.

It was only a rough sketch of Laurie taming a horse, and every line of the active figure, resolute face, and commanding attitude was full of energy and meaning, contrasting sharply with the languid grace of the new sketch. Laurie said nothing, but as his eye went from one to the other, Amy saw him flush up and fold his lips together as if he read and accepted the little lesson she had given him. That satisfied her, and without waiting for him to speak, she said, in her sprightly way, "Don't you remember the day you tamed Puck, and I sat on the fence and drew you. I found that sketch in my portfolio the other day, touched it up, and kept it to show you."

"Much obliged. You've improved immensely since then, and I congratulate you. May I venture to suggest that five o'clock is the dinner hour at your hotel?"

Laurie rose as he spoke, returned the pictures with a smile and a bow and looked at his watch. Amy felt the shade of coldness in his manner, and said to herself, "Now I've offended him. Well, if it does him good, I'm glad, and if it makes him hate me, I'm sorry. But it's true, and I can't take back a word of it."

They laughed and chatted all the way home, and little Baptiste, up behind, thought that monsieur and mademoiselle were in charming spirits. But despite their apparent gaiety, both felt ill at ease.

"Shall we see you this evening?" asked Amy, as they parted at her aunt's door.

"Unfortunately I have an engagement." And Laurie bent as if to kiss her hand, in European fashion.

Something in his face made Amy say quickly and warmly, "No, be yourself with me, Laurie."

"Goodbye, dear." And with these words, uttered in the tone she liked, Laurie left her, after a handshake almost painful in its heartiness.

Next morning, Amy received a note which made her smile at the beginning and sigh at the end:

My dear Teacher,
Please make my farewell to your aunt, and exult within yourself, for "Lazy Laurence" has gone to his grandpa, like the best of boys. A pleasant winter to you, and may the gods grant you a blissful honeymoon at Valrosa! I think Fred would be benefited by a rouser. Tell him so, with my congratulations.

Yours gratefully,
Laurie

    "Good boy! I'm glad he's gone," said Amy, with an approving smile. The next minute her face fell as she glanced about the empty room, adding, with an involuntary sigh, "Yes, I am glad, but how I shall miss him!"

17
THE VALLEY OF THE SHADOW

WHEN THE FIRST BITTERNESS WAS OVER, the family accepted the inevitable. They put away their grief, and each did his or her part toward making that last year a happy one.

The most pleasant room in the house was set apart for Beth, and in it was gathered everything that she most loved—flowers, pictures, her piano, the little worktable, and the beloved cats. Father's best books found their way there, Mother's easy chair, Jo's desk, Amy's finest sketches, and every day Meg brought her babies to make sunshine for Aunty Beth. John enjoyed the pleasure of keeping the invalid supplied with the fruit she loved, old Hannah never wearied of concocting dainty dishes, dropping tears as she worked, and from across the sea came little gifts and cheerful letters, like breaths of warmth and fragrance from lands that know no winter.

Beth was as tranquil and busy as ever, for nothing could change the sweet, unselfish nature. Even while preparing to leave life, she tried to make it happier for those who should remain behind. The feeble fingers were never idle, and one of her pleasures was to make little things for the schoolchildren daily passing to and fro—to drop a pair of mittens from her window for a pair of purple hands, a needlebook for some small mother of many dolls, scrapbooks for picture-loving eyes, and all manner of little things, till the children came to regard the gentle giver as a sort of fairy godmother who showered down gifts. If Beth had wanted any reward, she found it in the bright little faces always turned up to her window, with nods and smiles, and the droll little letters which came to her, full of blots and gratitude.

The first few months were happy ones. Beth often used to look round and say, "How beautiful this is!" as they all sat together in her sunny room, the babies kicking and crowing on the floor, mother and sisters working near, and father reading, in his pleasant voice, from wise old books which show that hope can comfort love, and faith make resignation possible.

This peaceful time was preparation for the sad hours to come. By-and-by, Beth said the needle was "so heavy," and put it down forever. Talking wearied her, faces troubled her, pain claimed her for its own. Such heavy days, such long, long nights, such aching hearts and imploring prayers, when those who loved her best were forced to see the thin hands stretched out to them beseechingly, to hear the bitter cry, "Help me, help me!" and to feel that there was no help. With the wreck of her frail body, Beth's soul grew strong, and though she said little, those about her felt that she was ready, and waited with her on the shore, trying to see the Shining Ones coming to receive her when she crossed the river.

Jo never left her for an hour since Beth had said, "I feel stronger when you are here." She slept on a couch in the room, waking often to renew the fire, to feed, lift, or wait upon the patient creature who seldom asked for anything, and "tried not to be a trouble." All day she haunted the room, prouder of being chosen than of any honor her life ever brought her. Now Jo's heart received the teaching that it needed: sweet lessons in patience that she could not fail to learn; charity for all, the lovely spirit that can forgive and truly forget unkindness, the loyalty to duty that makes the hardest easy, and the sincere faith that fears nothing, but trusts undoubtingly.

Often when she woke, Jo found Beth reading in her well-worn New

Testament or heard her singing softly to pass the sleepless night. Jo would lie watching her with thoughts too deep for tears, feeling that Beth, in her simple, unselfish way, was trying to fit herself for the life to come, with sacred words of comfort, quiet prayers, and the music she loved so well.

Seeing this did more for Jo than the wisest sermons, the saintliest hymns, the most fervent prayers that any voice could utter. With eyes made clear by many tears, and a heart softened by the tenderest sorrow, she recognized the beauty of her sister's life. In her loving unselfishness, Beth had achieved the true success which is possible to all.

One night as Beth turned the pages of her old favorite, *Pilgrim's Progress*, she found a little paper, scribbled over in Jo's hand. The blurred lines made her sure that tears had fallen on it.

"Poor Jo! She's fast asleep, so I won't wake her to ask her permission. She shows me all her things, and I don't think she'll mind if I look at this," thought Beth, with a glance at her sister, who lay on the rug.

MY BETH

Sitting patient in the shadow
    Till the blessed light shall come,
A serene and saintly presence
    Sanctifies our troubled home.
Earthly joys and hope and sorrows
    Break like ripples on the strand
Of the deep and solemn river
    Where her willing feet now stand.

O my sister, passing from me,
    Out of human care and strife,
Leave me, as a gift, those virtues
    Which have beautified your life.
Dear, bequeath me that great patience
    Which has power to sustain

A cheerful, uncomplaining spirit
In its prison-house of pain.

There were five stanzas, ending with these words:

Hope and faith, born of my sorrow,
Guardian angels shall become,
And the sister gone before me
By their hands shall lead me home.

Blurred and blotted, faulty and feeble as the lines were, they brought a look of inexpressible comfort to Beth. Her one regret had been that she had done so little, and this seemed to assure her that her life had not been useless. As she sat with the paper folded between her hands, the charred log fell apart. Jo started up, revived the blaze, and crept to the bedside, hoping Beth slept.

"Not asleep, but so happy. See, I found this and read it. I knew you wouldn't care. Have I been all that to you, Jo?" she asked, with wistful, humble earnestness.

"Oh, Beth, so much, so much!" And Jo's head went down upon the pillow beside her sister's.

"Then I don't feel as if I'd wasted my life. I'm not so good as you make me, but I have tried to do right. And now, when it's too late to begin even to do better, it's such a comfort to know that someone loves me so much, and feels as if I'd helped them."

"More than any one in the world, Beth. I used to think I couldn't let you go, but I'm learning to feel that I don't lose you. You'll be more to me than ever, and death can't part us, though it seems to."

"I know it cannot, and I don't fear it any longer, for I'm sure I shall be your Beth still, to love and help you more than ever. You must take my place, Jo, and be everything to Father and Mother when I'm gone. You'll be happier in doing that than writing splendid books or seeing all the world. Love is the only thing that we can carry with us when we go, and it makes the end so easy."

"I'll try, Beth."

So the spring days came and went, the sky grew clearer, the earth greener, the flowers were up fair and early, and the birds came back in time to say goodbye to Beth, who was like a tired but trustful child.

Seldom except in books do the dying utter memorable words, see visions, or depart with beautified faces. Those who have sped many parting souls know that to most the end comes as naturally and simply as sleep. As Beth had hoped, the "tide went out easily," and in the dark hour before the dawn, she quietly drew her last breath, with no farewell but one loving look, one little sigh.

When morning came, for the first time in many months the fire was out, Jo's place was empty, and the room was still. But a bird sang blithely on a budding bough close by, the snowdrops blossomed freshly at the window, and the spring sunshine streamed in like a benediction over the placid face upon the pillow—a face so full of painless peace that those who loved it best smiled through their tears, and thanked God that Beth was well at last.

18

LEARNING TO FORGET

AMY'S LECTURE DID LAURIE GOOD, though, of course, he did not admit it till long afterward—men seldom do. He went back to his grandfather, and the old gentleman declared the climate of Nice had improved him wonderfully, and he had better try it again. There was nothing the young gentleman would have liked better, but elephants could not have dragged him back after the scolding he had received. Whenever the longing grew strong, he fortified his resolution by repeating the words that had made the deepest impression, "I despise you." "Go and do something splendid that will make her love you."

Laurie soon brought himself to confess that he had been selfish and lazy, but his great sorrow was a good excuse. Jo wouldn't love him, but he might do something to make her respect and admire him. He had always meant to do something, and Amy's advice was unnecessary.

Laurie resolved to embalm his love sorrow in music, and compose a Requiem which should melt the heart of every hearer. Therefore the next time the old gentleman found him getting restless and ordered him off, he went to Vienna, where he had musical friends, and fell to work. But, whether the sorrow was too vast to be embodied in music, or music too ethereal to contain such woe, he soon discovered that the Requiem was beyond him just at present. Often in the middle of a somber passage, he would find himself humming a dance tune that vividly reminded him of the Christmas ball at Nice, which put a stop to tragic composition for the time being.

Then he tried an opera, for nothing seemed impossible in the beginning. He wanted Jo for his heroine, and romantic visions of his love. But he could recall only Jo's oddities, faults, and freaks. Jo wouldn't be put into the opera at any price, and he had to give her up, exclaiming, "What a torment she is!" and clutching at his hair, as became a distracted composer.

When he looked about him for a more cooperative female to immortalize, imagination produced one. This phantom wore many faces, but it always had golden hair and floated airily before his mind's eye in a pleasing chaos of roses, peacocks, white ponies, and blue ribbons. He did not give her any name, but took her for his heroine and grew fond of her, as well he might, for he gifted her with every grace under the sun, and escorted her, unscathed, through trials which would have annihilated any mortal woman.

Thanks to this inspiration, he got on very well for a time, but his mind seemed to be in an unsettled state that winter. "It's genius simmering, perhaps. I'll let it simmer, and see what comes of it," he said, with a secret suspicion all the while that it wasn't genius, but something far more common. Whatever it was, he finally came to the wise conclusion that not everyone who loved music was a composer. Returning from one of Mozart's grand operas, splendidly performed at the Royal Theatre, he looked over his own opera, played a few of the best parts, sat staring up at the busts of Mendelssohn, Beethoven, and Bach, who stared back. Then suddenly he tore up his music sheets, one by one, and as the last fluttered out of his hand, he said soberly to himself, "She is right! Talent isn't genius. Mozart has taken the vanity out of me as Rome took it out of her, and I won't be a humbug any longer. Now what shall I do?"

That seemed a hard question to answer, and Laurie began to wish he had to work for his daily bread. He had plenty of opportunity for "going to the devil," as he once expressed it, for he had plenty of money and nothing to do, and Satan makes fond use of full and idle hands. But his promise to his grandfather, and his desire to be able to look honestly into the eyes of the women who loved him and say "All's well," kept him safe and steady.

Laurie thought the task of forgetting his love for Jo would absorb all his powers for years, but to his great surprise he discovered it grew easier every day. His heart wouldn't ache. The wound persisted in healing with a rapidity that astonished him, and instead of trying to forget, he found himself trying to remember. He had not foreseen this turn of affairs, and was not prepared for it. He was surprised at his own fickleness, and full of a strange mixture of disappointment and relief that he could recover from such a tremendous blow so soon, leaving a brotherly affection.

As the word *brotherly* passed through his mind in one of these reveries, he smiled and glanced up at the picture of Mozart that was before him. "Well, he was a great musician, and when he couldn't have one sister he took the other, and was happy." The next instant he kissed the little old ring, saying to himself, "No, I won't! I haven't forgotten, I never can. I'll try again, and if that fails, why, then . . ."

Leaving his sentence unfinished, he seized pen and paper and wrote to Jo, telling her that he could not settle to anything while there was the least hope of her changing her mind. Couldn't she, wouldn't she, and let him come home and be happy? While waiting for an answer he did nothing, but he did it energetically. Jo's answer came at last: she couldn't and wouldn't. She was wrapped up in Beth, and never wished to hear the word love again. Then she begged him to be happy with somebody else, but always to keep a little corner of his heart for his loving sister Jo. In a postscript she desired him not to tell Amy that Beth was worse, but to write to her often, and not let her feel lonely, homesick, or anxious.

"So I will, at once. Poor little girl, it will be a sad going home for her, I'm afraid." And Laurie opened his desk.

But he did not write the letter that day, for as he rummaged out his best paper, he came across something which changed his purpose. Tumbling about in one part of the desk among bills, passports, and business documents of various kinds were several of Jo's letters, and in another compartment were three notes from Amy, carefully tied up with one of her blue ribbons. Laurie gathered up all Jo's letters, smoothed, folded, and put them neatly into a small drawer of the desk, stood a minute turning the ring thoughtfully on his finger, then slowly drew it off, laid it with the letters, locked the drawer, and went out, feeling as if there had been a funeral.

The letter went soon, however, and was promptly answered, for Amy was homesick, and confessed it in the most delightfully confiding manner. Letters flew to and fro with unfailing regularity all through the early spring. Laurie wanted desperately to go to Nice, but would not till he was asked, and Amy would not ask him, for just then she was having little experiences of her own, which made her wish to avoid his quizzical eyes.

Fred Vaughn had returned, and put the question to which she had once decided to answer, "Yes, thank you," but now she said, "No, thank you," kindly but steadily, for she found that something more than money and position was needed to satisfy her heart. The words, "Fred is a good fellow, but not at all the man I fancied you would ever like," and Laurie's face when he uttered them, kept returning to her. She didn't care to be a queen of society now half so much as she did to be a lovable woman.

Laurie's letters were such a comfort, for the letters from home were irregular, and were not half so cheerful as his when they did come. It was not only a pleasure but a duty to answer him, for the poor fellow was forlorn because of Jo. There was nothing to do but be kind and treat him like a brother.

If all brothers were treated as well as Laurie was at this period, they would be a much happier race of beings than they are. Amy never lectured now. She asked his opinion on all subjects, she was interested in everything he did, made charming little presents for him, and sent him two letters a week, full of lively gossip, sisterly confidences, and captivating sketches of the lovely scenes about her.

Few brothers have their letters carried about in their sisters' pockets, read and reread diligently, cried over when short, kissed when long, and treasured carefully. Amy went out sketching alone a good deal that spring. She never had much to show when she came home, but was studying nature, I dare say, while she sat for hours, with her hands folded, on the terrace at Valrosa, or absently sketched any fancy that occurred to her—a stalwart knight carved on a tomb or a young man asleep in the grass with his hat over his eyes.

Amy let Laurie know that Fred had gone to Egypt. That was all, but he understood it and looked relieved, as he said to himself, "I was sure she would think better of it. Poor old fellow! I've been through it all, and I can sympathize." With that he heaved a great sigh, and then, as if he had discharged his duty to the past, put his feet up on the sofa and enjoyed Amy's letter luxuriously.

The letter telling that Beth was failing never reached Amy, and when the next found her, the grass was green above her sister. The sad news met her in Switzerland, for the heat had driven them there in May. Her heart was heavy, she longed to be at home, and every day looked wistfully across the lake, waiting for Laurie to come and comfort her.

He did come soon, for the same mail brought letters to them both, but he was in Germany, and it took some days to reach him. The moment he read it, he packed his knapsack and was off to keep his promise, with a heart full of joy and sorrow, hope and suspense.

He knew Vevey well, and as soon as the boat touched the little quay, he hurried along the shore to La Tour, where the Carrols were living. The servant was in despair that the whole family had gone for a walk along the lake, but no, the blonde mademoiselle might be in the garden. If monsieur would wait a moment—but monsieur could not wait and in the middle of the speech departed to find mademoiselle himself.

Amy often came to the pleasant old garden to read or work, or console herself with the beauty all about her. She was sitting here that day with a homesick heart and heavy eyes, thinking of Beth and wondering why Laurie did not come. She did not hear him cross the courtyard beyond, nor see him pause in the archway that led from the subterranean path into the garden. He stood a minute, looking at her with new eyes, seeing what no one had ever seen before—the tender side of Amy's character. Everything about her mutely suggested love and sorrow—the tear-stained letters in her lap, the black ribbon that tied up her hair, the womanly pain in her face, even the little ebony cross at her throat which he had given to her. If he had any doubts about the reception she would give him, they were set at rest the minute she looked up and saw him, for dropping everything, she ran to him, exclaiming in a tone of unmistakable love and longing, "Oh, Laurie, Laurie, I knew you'd come to me!"

I think everything was settled then, for as they stood together silent for a moment, with the dark head bent down protectingly over the light one, Amy felt that no one could comfort and sustain her so well as Laurie, and Laurie decided that Amy was the only woman in the world who could fill Jo's place.

While Amy dried her tears, Laurie gathered up the scattered papers, finding in the well-worn letters and suggestive sketches good omens for the future. As he sat down beside her, Amy felt shy again, and turned rosy red at the recollection of her impulsive greeting. "I couldn't help it, I felt so lonely and sad, and was so glad to see you. I was beginning to fear you wouldn't come."

"I came the minute I heard. I wish I could say something to comfort you." He longed to lay Amy's head down on his shoulder, and tell her to have a good cry, but he did not dare. He took her hand instead, and gave it a sympathetic squeeze that was better than words.

"Beth is well and happy, and I mustn't wish her back. But I dread the going home, much as I long to see them all. We won't talk about it now, for it makes me cry, and I want to enjoy you while you stay. You needn't go right back, need you?"

"Not if you want me, dear."

"I do, so much. Aunt and Flo are kind, but you seem like one of the family."

"Poor little soul, you look as if you'd grieved yourself half sick! I'm going to take care of you, so don't cry any more, but come and walk about with me. The wind is too chilly for you to sit still," he said, in the half-caressing, half-commanding way that Amy liked, as he tied on her hat, drew her arm through his, and began to pace up and down the sunny walk. He felt more at ease upon his legs, and Amy found it pleasant to have a strong arm to lean upon, a familiar face to smile at her, and a kind voice to talk delightfully for her alone.

The quaint old garden had sheltered many pairs of lovers and seemed expressly made for them, so sunny and secluded was it, with nothing but the tower to overlook them and the wide lake to carry away the echo of their words as it rippled by below. For an hour this new pair walked and talked, or rested on the wall. When an unromantic dinner bell called them away, Amy felt as if she left her burden of loneliness and sorrow behind her in the garden.

The moment Mrs. Carrol saw the girl's altered face, she was illuminated with a new idea, and exclaimed to herself, "Now I understand it all. The child has been pining for young Laurence. Bless my heart, I never thought of such a thing!" The good lady said nothing and betrayed no sign of enlightenment, but cordially urged Laurie to stay.

At Nice, Laurie had lounged and Amy had scolded. At Vevey, Laurie was always walking, riding, boating, or studying in the most energetic manner, while Amy admired everything he did and followed his

166

example as far and as fast as she could.

The invigorating air did them both good, and much exercise worked wholesome changes in minds as well as bodies. They seemed to get clearer views of life and duty up there among the everlasting hills. The fresh winds blew away desponding doubts, delusive fancies, and moody mists, and the warm spring sunshine brought out all sorts of aspiring ideas, tender hopes, and happy thoughts. The lake seemed to wash away the troubles of the past, and the grand old mountains to look down upon them, saying, "Little children, love one another."

In spite of the new sorrow, it was a happy time, so happy that Laurie could not bear to disturb it by a word. He consoled himself for the seeming disloyalty to his first love by the thought that Jo's sister was almost the same as Jo's self. The new romance, he resolved, should be as calm and simple as possible. There was no need of having a scene, hardly any need of telling Amy that he loved her, she knew it without words and had given him his answer long ago. It all came about so naturally that no one could complain, and he knew that everybody would be pleased, even Jo. Laurie let the days pass, enjoying every hour, and leaving to chance the utterance of the word that would put an end to the first and sweetest part of his new romance.

He had imagined that the proposal would take place in the garden by moonlight, and in the most graceful and decorous manner. But it turned out exactly the reverse, for the matter was settled on the lake at noonday in a few blunt words. They had been floating about all the morning with a cloudless blue sky overhead, and the bluer lake below, dotted with the picturesque boats that look like white-winged gulls.

Amy had been dabbling her hand in the water during the little pause that fell between them, and when she looked up, Laurie was leaning on his oars with an expression in his eyes that made her say hastily, merely for the sake of saying something, "You must be tired. Rest a little, and let me row. It will do me good, for since you came I have been altogether lazy."

"I'm not tired, but you may take an oar, if you like. There's room enough, though I have to sit nearly in the middle," returned Laurie, as if he liked the arrangement.

Amy squeezed in next to him and accepted an oar. She rowed as well as she did many other things, and though she used both hands and Laurie but one, the oars kept time, and the boat went smoothly through the water.

"How well we pull together, don't we?" said Amy.

"So well that I wish we might always pull in the same boat. Will you, Amy?" very tenderly.

"Yes, Laurie," very low.

Then they both stopped rowing, and added a pretty little scene of human love and happiness to the dissolving views reflected in the lake.

19
ALL ALONE

SOME PEOPLE SEEMED TO GET ALL SUNSHINE, and some all shadow. It was not fair, thought Jo, for she got only disappointment, trouble, and hard work.

Poor Jo, these were dark days to her. "I can't do it. I wasn't meant for a life like this, and I know I shall break away and do something desperate if somebody doesn't come and help me," she said to herself, when she fell into the moody, miserable state of mind which often comes when strong wills have to yield to the inevitable.

Often she started up at night, thinking Beth called her. When the sight of the little empty bed made her cry with the bitter cry of an unsubmissive sorrow, "Oh, Beth, come back! Come back!" her mother came to comfort her, not with words only, but the patient tenderness that soothes by a touch.

One day Jo went to the study, and leaning over the good gray head lifted to welcome her with a tranquil smile, she said, humbly, "Father, talk to me as you did to Beth. I need it more than she did, for I'm all wrong."

"My dear, nothing can comfort me like this," he answered, with a falter in his voice, and both arms around her, as if he, too, needed help, and did not fear to ask it. Then, sitting in Beth's little chair close beside him, Jo told her troubles. He gave her the help she needed and both found consolation, for the time had come when they could talk together not only as father and daughter, but as man and woman, with mutual sympathy as well as mutual love. The parents who had taught one child to meet death without fear, were trying now to teach another to accept life.

Something of Beth's housewifely spirit seemed to linger round her little mop and the old brush that were never thrown away. As she used them, Jo found herself humming the songs Beth used to hum, imitating Beth's orderly ways and giving the little touches here and there that kept everything fresh and cozy, which was the first step toward making home happy. She didn't know it till Hannah said with an approving squeeze of the hand, "You thoughtful creature. You're determined we shan't miss that dear lamb ef you can help it. We don't say much, but we see it, and the Lord will bless you for't. See ef He don't."

Now if Jo had been the heroine of a moral storybook, she ought to have become saintly, renounced the world, and gone about doing good. But Jo wasn't a heroine, only a struggling human girl like hundreds of others, and she just acted out her nature, being sad, cross, listless, or energetic, as the mood suggested. It's highly virtuous to say we'll be good, but we can't do it all at once, and it takes a long, strong pull before some of us even get our feet set in the right way. Jo was learning to do her duty, and to feel unhappy if she did not. But to do it cheerfully—ah, that was another thing!

"Why don't you write? That always used to make you happy," said her mother once, when the desponding fit overshadowed Jo.

"I've no heart to write, and if I had, nobody cares for my things."

"We do. Write something for us, and never mind the rest of the world. Try it, dear, I'm sure it would do you good, and please us very much."

"I don't believe I can." But Jo got out her desk and began to overhaul her half-finished manuscripts.

An hour afterward her mother peeped in and there she was, scratching away, with her black pinafore on and an absorbed expression, which caused Mrs. March to smile and slip away, well pleased with the success of her suggestion. Jo never knew how it happened, but something got into that story that went straight to the hearts of those who read it. When her family had laughed and cried over it, her father sent it, much against her will, to one of the popular magazines, and to her utter surprise, it was not only paid for, but others requested. Letters from several persons, whose praise was honor, followed the appearance of the little story. Newspapers copied it, and strangers as well as friends admired it. For a small thing it was a great success, and Jo was more astonished than when her novel was commended and condemned all at once.

"I don't understand it. What can there be in a simple little story like that to make people praise it so?" she said, bewildered.

"There is truth in it, Jo, that's the secret. Humor and pathos make it alive, and you have found your style at last. You wrote with no thought of fame or money, and put your heart into it. You have had the bitter, now comes the sweet. Do your best, and enjoy your success."

"If there is anything good or true in what I write, it isn't mine. I owe it all to you and Mother and to Beth," said Jo, more touched by her father's words than by any amount of praise from the world.

So taught by love and sorrow, Jo wrote her little stories, and sent them away to make friends for themselves and her.

When Amy and Laurie wrote of their engagement, Mrs. March feared that Jo would find it difficult. But though Jo looked grave at first, she took it quietly and was full of hopes and plans for "the children" before she read the letter twice. It was a sort of written duet, wherein each glorified the other in loverlike fashion, pleasant to read and satisfactory to think of, for no one had any objection to make.

"Do you like it, Mother?" said Jo, as they laid down the sheets and looked at one another.

"Yes, I hoped it would be so, ever since Amy wrote that she had refused Fred. I felt sure then that something better than what you call the 'mercenary spirit' had come over her, and a hint here and there in her letters made me suspect that love and Laurie would win the day."

"How sharp you are, Marmee, and how silent! You never said a word to me."

"Mothers have need of sharp eyes and discreet tongues. I was half afraid to put the idea into your head, lest you should write and congratulate them before the thing was settled."

"I'm not the scatterbrain I was. You may trust me."

"I fancied it might pain you to learn that your Teddy loved anyone else. Lately I have thought that if he came back and asked again, you might, perhaps, feel like giving another answer. Forgive me, dear, I can't help seeing that you are lonely."

"No, Mother, it is better as it is, and I'm glad Amy has learned to love him. But you are right in one thing—I am lonely. Perhaps if Teddy had tried again, I might have said yes, not because I love him any more, but because I care more to be loved than when he went away. My heart is so elastic, it never seems full now, and I used to be quite contented with my family. I don't understand it."

"I do." And Mrs. March smiled her wise smile, as Jo turned back to read what Amy said of Laurie.

"It is so beautiful to be loved as Laurie loves me. He isn't sentimental, doesn't say much about it, but I see and feel it in all he says and does, and it makes me so happy and so humble that I don't seem to be the same girl I was. I never knew how good and generous and tender he was till now, for he lets me read his heart, and I find it full of noble impulses and hopes and purposes, and am so proud to know it's mine. Oh, Mother, I never knew how much like heaven this world could be, when two people love and live for one another!"

"And that's our cool, reserved, and worldly Amy! Truly, love does work miracles. How happy they must be!" And Jo laid the rustling sheets together with a careful hand, as one might shut the covers of a lovely romance, which holds the reader fast till the end comes, and he finds himself alone in the workaday world again. She longed for love.

By-and-by Jo roamed away upstairs, for it was rainy and she could not walk outside. Up in the garret stood four little wooden chests in a row, each marked with its owner's name, and each filled with relics of the childhood and girlhood ended now. Jo glanced into them, and when she came to her own, leaned her chin on the edge and stared absently at the chaotic collection, till a bundle of old exercise books caught her eye. She drew them out, turned them over, and relived that pleasant winter at kind Mrs. Kirke's. She had smiled at first, then she looked thoughtful, next sad, and when she came to a little message written in the Professor's hand, her lips began to tremble. The books slid out of her lap, and she sat looking at the friendly words as if they took a new meaning and touched a tender spot in her heart.

"Wait for me, my friend. I may be a little late, but I shall surely come."

"Oh, if he only would! So kind, so good, so patient with me always. My dear old Fritz, I didn't value him half enough when I had him. But now how I should love to see him, for everyone seems going away from me, and I'm all alone."

And holding the little paper fast, as if it were a promise yet to be fulfilled, Jo laid her head down and cried.

20
SURPRISES

TOMORROW WAS HER BIRTHDAY, and Jo was thinking how fast the years went by, how old she was getting, and how little she seemed to have accomplished—almost twenty-five and nothing to show for it. (Jo was mistaken in that. There was a good deal to show.)

"An old maid, that's what I'm to be. A literary spinster, with a pen for a husband, a family of stories for children, and twenty years from now a morsel of fame, perhaps. Well, I needn't be a sour saint nor a selfish sinner, but . . ." And there Jo sighed.

Thirty seems the end of all things to someone twenty-five, but it's not as bad as it looks. One can get on happily if one has something in one's self to fall back upon. At twenty-five, girls begin to talk about being old maids, but secretly resolve that they never will be. Don't laugh at the spinsters, dear girls, for the faded faces are beautiful in God's sight. Even the sad, sour sisters should be kindly dealt with.

Girls in their bloom should remember that they too will lose the blossom time. Rosy cheeks don't last forever, silver threads will come in the bonnie brown hair, and by-and-by, kindness and respect will be as sweet as love and admiration now.

Gentlemen, which means boys, be courteous to the old maids, no matter how poor and plain and prim, for the only chivalry worth having is that which respects the old, protects the feeble, and serves womankind, regardless of rank, age, or color.

Jo must have fallen asleep, for suddenly Laurie's ghost seemed to stand before her—a substantial, lifelike ghost. She stared up at him in startled silence. When he stooped and kissed her, she flew up, crying joyfully, "O my Teddy! O my Teddy!"

"Dear Jo, you are glad to see me, then?"

"Glad! My blessed boy, words can't express my gladness. Where's Amy?"

"Your mother has her down at Meg's. We stopped there on the way, and there was no getting my wife out of their clutches."

"Your what?" cried Jo, for Laurie uttered those two words with an unconscious pride and satisfaction.

"Oh, the dickens! Now I've done it." And he looked so guilty that Jo was down upon him like a flash.

"You've gone and got married!"

"Yes, please, but I never will again." And he went down upon his knees to beg forgiveness, with a face full of mischief, mirth, and triumph.

"Actually married?"

"Very much so, thank you."

"Mercy on us! What dreadful thing will you do next?" And Jo fell into her seat with a gasp.

"A not exactly complimentary congratulation," returned Laurie, beaming with satisfaction.

"What can you expect, when you take one's breath away, creeping in like a burglar, and letting cats out of bags like that? Get up, you ridiculous boy, and tell me all about it."

"Not a word, unless you let me come in my old place, and promise not to barricade."

Jo laughed at that as she had not done for many a long day, and patted the sofa invitingly, as she said in a cordial tone, "The old pillow is up in the garret, and we don't need it now. So, come and 'fess, Teddy."

"You've gone and got married!"

"How good it sounds to hear you say 'Teddy'! No one ever calls me that but you." And Laurie sat down with an air of great content.

"What does Amy call you?"

"My lord."

"That's like her. Well, you look it." And Jo's eye plainly betrayed that she found her boy handsomer than ever.

The pillow was gone, but there was a barricade, nevertheless—a natural one, raised by time, absence, and change of heart. Laurie said, with a vain attempt at dignity, "Don't I look like a married man and the head of a family?"

"Not a bit, and you never will. You are the same scapegrace as ever."

"Now, really, Jo, you ought to treat me with more respect," began Laurie, who enjoyed it all immensely.

"How can I, when the mere idea of you, married and settled, is so irresistibly funny that I can't keep sober?" answered Jo, smiling all over her face, so infectiously that they had another laugh, and then settled down for a good talk in the pleasant old fashion.

"It's no use your going out in the cold to get Amy, for they are all coming up presently. I couldn't wait. I wanted to be the one to tell you the grand surprise."

"Of course you did, and spoiled your story by beginning at the wrong end. Now, start right, and tell me how it all happened. I'm pining to know."

"Well, I did it to please Amy," began Laurie, with a twinkle that made Jo exclaim, "Fib number one. Amy did it to please you. Go on, and tell the truth, if you can, sir."

"It's all the same, you know, she and I being one. The Carrols decided to pass another winter in Paris. But Grandpa wanted to come home, and I couldn't let him go alone, neither could I leave Amy. Mrs. Carrol wouldn't let Amy come with us, so I just settled the difficulty by saying, 'Let's be married, and then we can do as we like.' "

"Of course you did. You always have things to suit you."

"Not always." And something in Laurie's voice made Jo say hastily, "How did you ever get Aunt to agree?"

"It was hard work, but between us we talked her over, for we had heaps of good reasons on our side. It was only 'taking Time by the fetlock,' as my wife says."

"Aren't we proud of those two words, and don't we like to say them?" interrupted Jo, watching with delight the happy light in the eyes that had been so tragically gloomy when she saw them last.

"A trifle, perhaps, she's such a captivating little woman I can't help being proud of her. Well, that charming arrangement would make everything easy all round, so we did it."

"When, where, how?" asked Jo, in a fever of feminine curiosity.

"Six weeks ago, at the American consul's, in Paris. A quiet wedding, of course, for even in our happiness we didn't forget dear little Beth." Jo put her hand in his as he said that.

"Why didn't you let us know afterward?" asked Jo, in a quieter tone, when they had sat still a minute.

"We wanted to surprise you. We thought we were coming directly home at first, but the dear old gentleman, as soon as we were married, found he couldn't be ready under a month, at least, and sent us off to spend our honeymoon wherever we liked. Amy had once called Valrosa a regular honeymoon home, so we went there, and were as happy as people are but once in their lives. Wasn't it love among the roses!"

Laurie seemed to forget Jo for a minute, and Jo was glad of it, for the fact that he told her these things so freely and naturally assured her that he had forgiven her. She tried to draw away her hand, but Laurie held it fast.

"Jo, dear, I want to say one thing, and then we'll put it by forever. Amy and you changed places in my heart. I think it was meant to be so, and would have come about naturally, if I had waited, as you tried to make me; but I never could be patient. For it was a mistake, Jo, as you said, and I found it out after making a fool of myself. When I saw Amy in Switzerland, everything seemed to clear up all at once. You both got into your right places, and I felt sure that I could honestly share my heart between sister Jo and wife Amy, and love them both dearly. Will you believe it, and go back to the happy old times when we first knew one another?"

"I'll believe it, with all my heart. But Teddy, we never can be boy and girl again. I shall miss my boy, but I shall love the man as much and admire him more because he means to be what I hoped he would. We can't be little playmates any longer, but we will be brother and sister, to love and help one another all our lives, won't we, Laurie?"

He did not say a word, but took the hand she offered him, and laid his face down on it for a minute, feeling that out of the grave of a boyish passion there had risen a beautiful, strong friendship to bless them both. Presently Jo said cheerfully, for she didn't want the coming home to be a sad one, "I can't make it true that you children are really married. It seems only yesterday that I was buttoning Amy's pinafore and pulling your hair when you teased. Mercy me, how time does fly!"

"As one of the children is older than yourself, you needn't talk so like a grandma."

"You may be a little older in years, but I'm ever so much older in feeling, Teddy. Women always are, and this last year has been such a hard one that I feel forty."

"Poor Jo! We left you to bear it alone while we went pleasuring. You are older—here's a line, and there's another. Unless you smile, your eyes look sad, and when I touched the cushion just now, I felt tears on it. You've had a great deal to bear and had to bear it all alone. What a selfish beast I've been!" And Laurie pulled his own hair, with a remorseful look.

But Jo only turned over the telltale pillow and answered in a tone she tried to make cheerful, "No, I had Father and Mother to help me, the dear babies to comfort me, and the thought that you and Amy were safe and happy to make the troubles here easier to bear. I am lonely, sometimes, but I dare say it's good for me."

"You never shall be again," broke in Laurie, putting his arm about her, as if to fence out every human ill. "Amy and I can't get on without you, so you must come and teach us to keep house, and go halves in everything, just as we used to do, and all be blissfully happy and friendly together."

"If I shouldn't be in the way, it would be very pleasant. I begin to feel young already, for somehow all my troubles seemed to fly away when you came. You always were a comfort, Teddy." And Jo leaned her head on his shoulder, just as she did years ago, when Beth lay ill and Laurie told her to hold on to him.

He looked down at her, wondering if she remembered the time, but Jo was smiling to herself, as if her troubles had all vanished at his coming.

"You are the same Jo still, dropping tears about one minute, and laughing the next. You look a little wicked now. What is it, Grandma?"

"I was wondering how you and Amy get on together."

"Like angels!"

"Yes, of course, at first, but which rules?"

"I don't mind telling you that she does, now, at least I let her think so—it pleases her, you know. By-and-by we shall take turns, for marriage, they say, halves one's rights and doubles one's duties."

"You'll go on as you begin, and Amy will rule you all the days of your life."

"Well, she does it so smoothly that I don't think I shall mind much. She is the sort of woman who knows how to rule well. I rather like it, for she winds one round her finger as softly and prettily as a skein of silk, and makes you feel as if she was doing you a favor all the while."

"That ever I should live to see you a henpecked husband and enjoying it!" cried Jo, with uplifted hands.

It was good to see Laurie square his shoulders and smile with masculine scorn at that insinuation, as he replied, "My wife and I respect ourselves and one another too much ever to tyrannize or quarrel."

"I am sure of that. Amy and you never did quarrel as we used to. She is the sun and I the wind, in the fable, and the sun managed the man best, you remember."

"She can burn him as well as shine on him," laughed Laurie. "Such a lecture as I got at Nice! I give you my word it was a deal worse than any of your scoldings—a regular rouser. I'll tell you all about it sometime—she never will, because after telling me that she despised and was ashamed of me, she lost her heart to the despicable party and married the good-for-nothing."

"What baseness! Well, if she abuses you, come to me, and I'll defend you."

"I look as if I needed it, don't I?" said Laurie, getting up and striking an attitude which suddenly changed from the imposing to the rapturous, as Amy's voice was heard calling, "Where is she? Where's my dear old Jo?"

In trooped the whole family, and everyone was hugged and kissed all over again. Mr. Laurence, hale and hearty as ever, was as much improved as the others by his foreign tour. It was good to see him beam at "my children," as he called the young pair. It was better still to see Amy pay him the daughterly duty and affection which completely won his old heart. Best of all was to watch Laurie revolve about the two, as if never tired of enjoying the pretty picture they made.

The minute she put her eyes upon Amy, Meg became conscious that her own dress hadn't a Parisian air, that young Mrs. Moffat would be entirely eclipsed by young Mrs. Laurence, and that "her ladyship" was altogether a most elegant and graceful woman. Jo thought, as she watched the pair, "How well they look together! I was right, and Laurie has found the beautiful, accomplished girl who will become his home better than clumsy old Jo, and be a pride, not a torment to him." Mrs. March and her husband smiled and nodded at each other with happy faces, for they saw that their youngest had done well, not only in worldly things, but the better wealth of love, confidence, and happiness.

For Amy's face was full of the soft brightness which reveals a peaceful heart, her voice had a new tenderness in it, and the cool, prim carriage was changed to a gentle dignity, both womanly and winning. The cordial sweetness of her manner was more charming, for it stamped her at once with the unmistakable sign of the true gentlewoman she had hoped to become.

"Love has done much for our little girl," said her mother softly.

"She has had a good example before her all her life, my dear," Mr. March whispered back, with a loving look at the worn face and gray head beside him.

Daisy found it impossible to keep her eyes off her "pity aunty," but attached herself like a lap dog. Demi hung back suspiciously, however, and resisted a bribe, which took the tempting form of a family of wooden bears from Berne, Switzerland. But Laurie knew how to handle him.

"Young man, when I first had the honor of making your acquaintance you hit me in the face," and with that the tall uncle proceeded to toss and tousle the small nephew in a way that delighted him.

"Blest if she ain't in silk from head to foot! Ain't it a relishin sight to see her settin there as fine as a fiddle, and hear folks calling little Amy, Mis. Laurence?" muttered old Hannah as she set the table.

How they did talk! First one, then the other, then all burst out together, trying to tell the history of three years in half an hour. It was fortunate that tea was at hand to produce a lull and provide refreshment, for they would have been hoarse and faint if they had gone on much longer. Such a happy procession as filed away into the little dining room! Mr. March proudly escorted "Mrs. Laurence." Mrs. March as proudly leaned on the arm of "my son." The old gentleman took

Jo, with a whispered, "You must be my girl now," and a glance at the empty corner by the fire, that made Jo whisper back, with trembling lips, "I'll try to fill her place, sir."

The twins pranced behind, feeling that the millennium was at hand, for everyone was so busy with the newcomers that they were left to their own devices. You may be sure they made the most of the opportunity. Didn't they steal sips of tea, stuff gingerbread, get a hot biscuit apiece, and, as a crowning trespass, whisk a captivating little tart into their tiny pockets, there to stick and crumble treacherously, teaching them that both human nature and pastry are frail?

As everyone filed back up to the sitting room, Jo lingered to answer Hannah's eager question, "Will Miss Amy use all them lovely silver dishes that's stored away over yander?"

"Shouldn't wonder if she drove six white horses, ate off gold plate, and wore diamonds and point lace every day. Teddy thinks nothing too good for her," returned Jo with infinite satisfaction.

"No more there is! Will you have hash or fishballs for breakfast?" asked Hannah, who wisely mingled poetry and prose.

"I don't care," Jo said, and as Demi's short plaid legs toiled up the last stair, a sudden sense of loneliness came over her. If she had known what birthday gift was coming every minute nearer and nearer, she would not have said to herself, "I'll have a little cry when I go to bed. It won't do to be dismal now." Then she drew her hand over eyes—for one of her boyish habits was never to know where her handkerchief was—and had just managed to call up a smile when there came a knock at the porch door.

She opened it with hospitable haste, and started as if another ghost had come to surprise her. There stood a tall bearded gentleman, beaming on her from the darkness like a midnight sun.

"Oh, Mr. Bhaer, I am so glad to see you!" cried Jo as if she feared the night would swallow him up before she could get him in.

"And I to see Miss Marsch. But no, you haf a party . . ." And the

Professor paused as the sound of voices and the tap of dancing feet came down to them.

"No, we haven't, only the family. My sister and friends have just come home, and we are all happy. Do come in and join us."

Though a social man, Mr. Bhaer would have gone politely away and come back another day. But how could he, when Jo shut the door behind him and took his hat? Perhaps her face had something to do with it, for she forgot to hide her joy at seeing him and showed it with a frankness that proved irresistible, her welcome far exceeding his boldest hopes.

"I will so gladly see them all. You haf been ill, my friend?"

He put the question abruptly, for, as Jo hung up his coat, the light fell on her face, and he saw a change in it.

"Not ill, but tired and sorrowful. We have had trouble since I saw you last."

"Ah, yes, I know. My heart was sore for you when I heard that." And he shook hands again, with such a sympathetic face that Jo felt as if no comfort could equal the look of the kind eyes, the grasp of the big, warm hand.

"Father, Mother, this is my friend, Professor Bhaer," she said, with a face and tone of such pride and pleasure that she might as well have blown a trumpet and opened the door with a flourish.

Everyone greeted him kindly, for Jo's sake at first, but soon they liked him for his own, feeling even the more friendly because he was poor. Poverty enriches those who live above it and is a sure passport to truly hospitable spirits. Mr. Bhaer sat looking about him with the air of a traveler who knocks at a strange door, and, when it opens, finds himself at home. The children went to him like bees to a honeypot, and establishing themselves on each knee, proceeded to captivate him by rifling his pockets, pulling his beard, and investigating his watch, with juvenile audacity. The women telegraphed their approval to one another, and Mr. March, sensing a kindred spirit, opened his choicest stores for his guest's benefit. Silent John listened and enjoyed the talk, but said not a word, and Mr. Laurence found it impossible to go to sleep.

If Jo had not been otherwise engaged, Laurie's behavior would have amused her, for a faint twinge, not of jealousy but something like suspicion, caused him to stand aloof at first and observe the newcomer with brotherly caution. But it did not last long. He got interested in spite of himself and, before he knew it, was drawn into the circle. Mr. Bhaer talked well in this genial atmosphere, and did himself justice. He seldom spoke to Laurie, but he looked at him often, and a shadow would pass across his face, as if regretting his own lost youth, as he watched the young man in his prime. Then his eye would turn to Jo so wistfully that she would have surely answered the mute inquiry if she had seen it. But Jo had her own eyes to take care of, and, feeling that they could not be trusted, she prudently kept them on the little sock she was knitting, like a model maiden aunt.

A stealthy glance now and then refreshed her like sips of fresh water after a dusty walk, for Mr. Bhaer's face had lost the absent-minded expression and looked all alive with interest in the present moment— actually young and handsome, she thought. Then he seemed inspired, though the burial customs of the ancients, to which the conversation had strayed, might not be considered an exhilarating topic. Jo glowed with triumph when Teddy got quenched in an argument, and thought to herself, as she watched her father's absorbed face, "How he would enjoy having such a man as my Professor to talk with every day!" Lastly, Mr. Bhaer was dressed in a new suit of black, which made him look more like a gentleman than ever. Poor Jo, how she did glorify that plain man as she sat knitting away so quietly, yet letting nothing escape her, not even the fact that Mr. Bhaer actually had gold sleeve-buttons in his immaculate wristbands.

"Dear old fellow! He couldn't have got himself up with more care if he'd been going a-wooing," said Jo to herself, and then a sudden thought born of the words made her blush so dreadfully that she had to drop her ball and go down after it to hide her face.

The maneuver did not succeed as well as she expected, however, for though just in the act of setting fire to a funeral pile, the Professor dropped his torch, so to speak, and made a dive after the little blue ball. Of course they bumped their heads smartly together, and both came up flushed and laughing, without the ball, to resume their seats, wishing they had not left them.

Nobody knew where the evening went, for Hannah skillfully abstracted the babies at an early hour, nodding like two rosy poppies, and Mr. Laurence went home to rest. The others sat around the fire, talking away, utterly regardless of the time, till Meg, whose maternal mind was impressed with a firm conviction that Daisy might have tumbled out of bed, made a move to go.

"We must have our sing, in the good old way, for we are all together again once more," said Jo, feeling that a good shout would be a safe and pleasant vent for the jubilant emotions of her soul.

They were not all there. But no one found the words thoughtless or untrue, for Beth still seemed among them, a peaceful presence, invisible, but dearer than ever. The little chair stood in its old place. The tidy basket, with the bit of work she left unfinished when the needle grew "so heavy," was still on its accustomed shelf. The beloved piano, seldom touched now, had not been moved, and above it Beth's face, serene and smiling, as in the early days, looked down upon them, seeming to say, "Be happy. I am here."

"Play something, Amy. Let them hear how much you have improved," said Laurie, with pardonable pride in his promising pupil.

But Amy whispered, with full eyes, as she twirled the faded stool, "Not tonight, dear. I can't show off tonight."

But she did show something better than brilliancy or skill, for she sang Beth's songs with a tender music in her voice which the best master could not have taught, and touched the listeners' hearts with a

186

sweeter power than any other inspiration could have given her. The room was still when the clear voice failed suddenly at the last line of Beth's favorite hymn. It was hard to say,

Earth hath no sorrow that heaven cannot heal

and Amy leaned against her husband, who stood behind her, feeling that her welcome home was not quite perfect without Beth's kiss.

"Now, we must finish with Mignon's song, for Mr. Bhaer sings that," said Jo, before the pause grew painful. And Mr. Bhaer cleared his throat with a gratified "Hem!" as he stepped into the corner where Jo stood, saying, "You will sing with me? We go excellently well together."

A pleasing fiction, for Jo had no more idea of music than a grasshopper. But she would have consented if he had proposed to sing a whole opera, and warbled away, blissfully regardless of time and tune. It didn't much matter, for Mr. Bhaer sang like a true German, heartily and well, and Jo soon subsided into a subdued hum, that she might listen to the mellow voice that seemed to sing for her alone.

The song was a great success, but a few minutes afterward the singer forgot his manners entirely and stared at Amy putting on her bonnet, for she had been introduced simply as "my sister," and no one had called her by her new name since he came. He forgot himself still further when Laurie said, in his most gracious manner, at parting, "My wife and I are glad to meet you, sir. Please remember that there is always a welcome waiting for you next door."

Then the Professor thanked him so heartily, and looked so suddenly illuminated with satisfaction, that Laurie thought him the most delightfully demonstrative old fellow he ever met.

"I too shall go. But I shall gladly come again, if you will gif me leave, dear madame, for a little business in the city will keep me here some days." He spoke to Mrs. March, but he looked at Jo.

"I suspect that is a wise man," remarked Mr. March, with placid satisfaction after the last guest had gone.

"I know he is a good one," added Mrs. March, with decided approval, as she wound up the clock.

"I thought you'd like him," was all Jo said, as she slipped away to her bed.

She wondered what the business was that brought Mr. Bhaer to the city, and finally decided that he had been appointed to some great honor, but had been too modest to mention the fact. If she had seen his face when, safe in his own room, he looked at the picture of a certain young lady, it might have thrown some light upon the subject—especially when he turned off the light and kissed the picture in the dark.

21

MY LORD AND LADY

"PLEASE MADAM MOTHER, could you lend me my wife for half an hour? The luggage has come, and I've been making hay of Amy's Paris finery, trying to find some things I want. I can't get on without my little woman any more than a . . ."

"Weathervane can without wind," suggested Jo, who had grown her own saucy self again since Teddy came home.

"Exactly, for Amy keeps me pointing due west most of the time, and I am altogether balmy—right, my lady?"

"Lovely weather so far, though I don't know how long it will last. Come home, dear, and I'll find your bootjack so you can take off your boot. I suppose that's what you want. Men are so helpless, Mother," said Amy.

"What are you going to do with yourselves after you get settled?" asked Jo, buttoning Amy's cloak as she used to button her pinafores.

"We have our plans. We don't mean to say much about them yet, but we don't intend to be idle. I'm going into business and prove to Grandfather that I'm not spoiled. I need something of the sort to keep me steady. I'm tired of dawdling and mean to work like a man."

"And Amy, what is she going to do?" asked Mrs. March.

"We shall astonish you by the elegant hospitalities of our mansion, the brilliant society we shall draw about us, and the beneficial influence we shall exert over the world at large. That's about it, isn't it?" asked Laurie, with a quizzical look at Amy.

"Time will show," answered Amy, resolving that there should be a home with a good wife in it before she became a queen of society.

"I think it will last," said Mrs. March after they left, with the restful expression of a pilot who has brought a ship safely into port.

"I know it will. Happy Amy!" And Jo sighed, then smiled brightly as Professor Bhaer opened the gate with an impatient push.

Later in the evening, when his mind had been set at rest about the bootjack, Laurie said suddenly to his wife, who was flitting about, arranging her new art treasures, "Mrs. Laurence."

"My lord?"

"That man intends to marry our Jo! I do wish he was a little younger and a good deal richer."

"Now, Laurie, if they love one another it doesn't matter a particle how old they are nor how poor. Women never should marry for money—"

Amy caught herself up short as the words escaped her, and looked at her husband, who replied, "Certainly not, though you do hear charming girls say that they intend to do it sometimes. If my memory serves me, you once thought it your duty to make a rich match. That accounts, perhaps, for your marrying a good-for-nothing like me."

"Oh, my dearest boy, don't, don't say that! I forgot you were rich when I said yes. I'd have married you if you hadn't a penny, and I sometimes wish you were poor that I might show how much I love you." And Amy, who was dignified in public and affectionate in private, gave convincing proofs of her sincerity. "It would break my heart if you didn't believe that I'd gladly pull in the same boat with you, even if you had to get your living by rowing on the lake."

"Am I an idiot and a brute? How could I think so, when you refused a richer man for me, and won't let me give you half I want to now? You were true to your mother's teaching. I told Mamma so yesterday, and she looked as glad as if I'd given her a check for a million, to be spent in charity. You are not listening, Mrs. Laurence." And Laurie paused, for Amy's eyes had an absent look, though fixed upon his face.

"Yes, I am, and admiring the dimple in your chin at the same time. I don't wish to make you vain, but I must confess that I'm prouder of my handsome husband than of all his money. Don't laugh, but your nose is such a comfort to me." And Amy softly caressed the well-cut feature with artistic satisfaction. "May I ask you a question, dear?"

"Of course you may."

"Shall you care if Jo does marry Mr. Bhaer?"

"Oh, that's the trouble, is it? I assure you I can dance at Jo's wedding with a heart as light as my heels. Do you doubt it, my darling?"

Amy looked up at him and was satisfied. Her last little jealous fear vanished forever, and she thanked him, with a face full of love and confidence.

"I wish we could do something for that capital old Professor. Couldn't we invent a rich relation, who shall obligingly die out there in Germany, and leave him a tidy little fortune?" said Laurie, when they began to pace up and down the long drawing room, arm in arm, as they were fond of doing in memory of the chateau garden.

"Jo would find out and spoil it all. She is proud of him, just as he is, and said yesterday that she thought poverty was a beautiful thing."

"Bless her dear heart! She won't think so when she has a dozen little professors and professorins to support. We won't interfere now, but watch our chance, and do them a good turn in spite of themselves. I owe Jo for a part of my education, and she believes in people's paying their honest debts, so I'll get round her some way."

"How delightful it is to be able to help others, isn't it? That was always one of my dreams, to have the power of giving freely."

"Ah, we'll do quantities of good, won't we? There's one sort of poverty that I particularly like to help. Out-and-out beggars get taken care of, but well-to-do folks who have fallen on hard times fare badly because people don't dare to offer charity. Yet there are a thousand ways of helping them, if one only knows how to do it."

"It takes a gentleman to do it."

"Thank you, I'm afraid I don't deserve that pretty compliment. But I was going to say that while I was dawdling about abroad, I saw a good many talented young fellows making all sorts of sacrifices and enduring real hardships, pursuing their dreams—so full of courage and ambition that I was ashamed of myself. Those are people it's a satisfaction to help."

"Yes, and there's another class who can't ask, and who suffer in silence. I know something of it, for I belonged to it before you made a princess of me, as the king does the beggarmaid in the old story. Ambitious girls have a hard time, Laurie, and often have to see youth, health, and precious opportunities go by, just for want of a little help at the right minute. Whenever I see girls struggling along, I want to put out my hand and help them, as I was helped."

"And so you shall, like the angel you are!" cried Laurie, resolving to found and endow an institution for the express benefit of young women with artistic tendencies. "Rich people have no right to let their money accumulate for others to waste. It's not half so sensible to leave legacies when one dies as it is to use the money wisely while alive, and enjoy making one's fellow creatures happy with it. We'll have a good time ourselves and add an extra relish to our own pleasure by giving other people a generous taste."

So the young pair shook hands upon it, and then paced happily on again, feeling that their pleasant home was more homelike because they hoped to brighten other homes.

22
DAISY AND DEMI

OF COURSE DAISY AND DEMI were the most remarkable children ever born—they walked at eight months, talked fluently at twelve months, and at two years they took their places at the table and charmed all beholders. At three, Daisy demanded a "needler," and actually made a bag with four stitches in it, while Demi learned his letters with his grandfather, who invented a new mode of teaching the alphabet by forming the letters with his arms and legs.

Demi developed a mechanical genius which delighted his father and distracted his mother, for he tried to imitate every machine he saw and kept the nursery in a chaotic condition with his "sewin-sheen," a mysterious structure of string, chairs, clothespins, and spools, for wheels to go "wound and wound." He also hung a basket over the back of a chair, in which he vainly tried to hoist his sister, explaining, "Dat's my lellywaiter."

Though utterly unlike in character, the twins got on remarkably well together and seldom quarreled more than three times a day. Of course, Demi tyrannized Daisy and gallantly defended her from every other aggressor, while Daisy made a galley slave of herself and adored her brother as the one perfect being in the world. A rosy, chubby, sun-shiny little soul was Daisy, who found her way to everybody's heart, and nestled there. She would have been angelic if a few small naughtinesses had not kept her human. Every morning she scrambled up to the window in her little nightgown to look out and say, no matter whether it rained or shone, "Oh, pitty day, oh, pitty day!" Everyone was a friend, and she offered kisses to strangers.

"Me loves everybody," she once said, opening her arms, with her spoon in one hand and her mug in the other, as if eager to embrace and nourish the whole world. Her grandfather accidentally called her "Beth," and her grandmother watched over her with untiring devotion, as if trying to atone for some past mistake, which no eye but her own could see.

Demi was always asking "What for?" One day he asked, "What makes my legs go, Dranpa?"

"It's your little mind, Demi," he replied, stroking the yellow head respectfully.

"What is a little mine?"

"It is something which makes your body move, as the spring made the wheels go in my watch when I showed it to you."

"Open me. I want to see it go wound."

"I can't do that. God winds you up, and you go till He stops you."

Demi's brown eyes grew big and bright. "Is I wounded up like the watch?"

"Yes, but I can't show you how, for it is done when we don't see."

Demi gravely remarked, "I dess Dod does it when I's asleep."

His anxious grandmother said, "My dear, do you think it wise to talk about such things to that baby?"

"If he is old enough to ask the question he is old enough to receive true answers. I am not putting the thoughts into his head but helping him unfold those already there. These children are wiser than we are, and I have no doubt the boy understands every word I have said to him. Now, Demi, where do you keep your mind?"

Demi answered, in a tone of calm conviction, "In my little tummy." Mr. March could only join in Grandma's laugh, and dismiss the class in metaphysics.

Meg made many moral rules and tried to keep them. "No more raisins, Demi, they'll make you sick," says Mamma to the young person who offers his services in the kitchen with unfailing regularity on plum-pudding day.

"Me likes to be sick."

Jo—Aunt Dodo—was chief playmate of both children, and the trio turned the little house topsy-turvy. Aunt Amy was as yet only a name to them, Aunt Beth soon faded into a pleasantly vague memory, but Aunt Dodo was a living reality, and they made the most of her. When Mr. Bhaer came, dismay and desolation fell upon their little souls. Daisy, who was fond of going about peddling kisses, lost her best customer. Demi soon discovered that Dodo liked to play with the "bearman" better than she did with him.

Though hurt, Demi concealed his anguish, for he hadn't the heart to insult a rival who kept a mine of chocolate drops in his waistcoat pocket. Daisy bestowed her small affections upon him at the third call, and considered his shoulder her throne, his arm her refuge, his gifts treasures of surpassing worth.

Mr. Bhaer was at home with children, and looked particularly well when little faces made a pleasant contrast with his manly one. His business, whatever it was, detained him from day to day, but evening seldom failed to bring him out to see—well, he always asked for Mr. March, so I suppose Mr. March was the attraction. The excellent papa labored under the delusion that he was, and enjoyed long discussions with the kindred spirit, till a chance remark of his grandson suddenly enlightened him.

Mr. Bhaer came in one evening to pause on the threshold of the study, astonished by the spectacle that met his eye. Prone upon the floor lay Mr. March, with his respectable legs in the air. Beside him was Demi, trying to imitate the position with his own short legs. Both were so seriously absorbed that they were unconscious of spectators, till Mr. Bhaer laughed, and Jo cried out, with a scandalized face,

"Father, Father, here's the Professor!"

Down went the black legs and up came the gray head, as Mr. March said, with undisturbed dignity, "Good evening, Mr. Bhaer. Excuse me for a moment—we are just finishing our lesson. Now, Demi, make the letter and tell its name."

After a few convulsive efforts, the little legs took the right shape, and the pupil triumphantly shouted, "It's a We, Dranpa, it's a We!" He was soon up and exploring the Professor's waistcoat pocket.

"Sweets for the sweet," Mr. Bhaer said to Demi with a kiss, and also offered Jo some of the chocolate, with a look that made her wonder if chocolate was not the nectar of the gods. Demi was impressed and innocently demanded, "Kiss Dodo too, 'Fessor?"

Mr. Bhaer gave a vague reply in a tone that made Mr. March put down his clothesbrush, glance at Jo's face, and then sink into his chair.

Why Jo, when she caught Demi in the pantry half an hour afterward, nearly squeezed the breath out of his little body with a tender embrace, instead of shaking him for being there, and why she followed up this performance by the unexpected gift of a big slice of bread and jelly, remained one of the problems over which Demi puzzled his small wits, and was forced to leave unsolved forever.

23

UNDER THE UMBRELLA

WHILE LAURIE AND AMY were strolling over velvet carpets, setting their house in order, Mr. Bhaer and Jo were strolling along muddy roads and sodden fields.

"I always do take a walk toward evening, and I don't know why I should give it up, just because I often happen to meet the Professor," said Jo to herself, after two or three encounters. Though there were two paths to Meg's, whichever one she took she was sure to meet him, either going or returning. He was always walking rapidly, and never seemed to see her till quite close. Then, if she was going to Meg's, he always had something for the babies. If her face was turned homeward, he had merely strolled down to see the river and could walk her home, unless they were tired of his frequent calls.

Under the circumstances, what could Jo do but greet him civilly and invite him in? If she was tired of his visits, she concealed her weariness with perfect skill and took care that there should be coffee for supper, "as Friedrich—I mean Mr. Bhaer—doesn't like tea."

By the second week, everyone knew perfectly well what was going on, yet everyone tried to look as if they were stone-blind to the changes in Jo's face. They never asked why she sang during her work and did up her hair three times a day. No one seemed to have the slightest suspicion that Professor Bhaer, while talking philosophy with the father, was giving the daughter lessons in love.

Laurie never alluded in the remotest manner to Jo's improved appearance, or expressed the least surprise at seeing the Professor's hat on the Marches' hall table nearly every evening. But he exulted in private and longed for the time to come when he could give Jo a piece of silverplate, with a bear on it as an appropriate coat of arms.

For two weeks the Professor came and went with loverlike regularity. Then he stayed away for three whole days, which caused everybody to look sober, and Jo to become pensive, at first, and then—alas for romance!—very cross.

"Disgusted, I dare say, and gone home as suddenly as he came. It's nothing to me, of course, but I should think he would have come and bid us goodbye like a gentleman," she said to herself, with a despairing look at the gate, as she put on her things for the customary walk one dull afternoon.

"You'd better take the little umbrella, dear. It looks like rain," said her mother, observing that she had on her new bonnet, but not mentioning the fact.

"Yes, Marmee, do you want anything in town? I've got to run in and get some paper," returned Jo, pulling out the bow under her chin before the glass as an excuse for not looking at her mother.

"Yes, I want some twilled lining fabric, a packet of number nine needles, and two yards of narrow lavender ribbon. Have you got your thick boots on and something warm under your cloak?"

"I believe so," answered Jo absently.

"If you happen to meet Mr. Bhaer, bring him home to tea. I long to see the dear man," added Mrs. March.

Jo made no answer except to kiss her mother and walk rapidly away, thinking with a glow of gratitude, in spite of her heartache, "How good she is to me! What do girls do who haven't any mothers to help them through their troubles?"

The dry-goods stores were not down among the banks and wholesale warehouses where gentlemen congregated. But Jo found herself in that part of the city before she did a single errand, loitering along as if waiting for someone, examining engineering instruments in one window and samples of wool in another. A drop of rain on her cheek drew her attention from baffled hopes to ruined ribbons, for the drops continued to fall, and she felt that although it was too late to save her heart, she might save her bonnet. Now she remembered the little umbrella, which she had forgotten to take in her hurry to be off. She looked up at the lowering sky, down at the crimson bow already flecked with black, forward along the muddy street, then one long, lingering look behind, at a certain grimy warehouse with the German name "Hoffmann, Swartz, & Co." over the door.

"It serves me right! What business had I to put on all my best things and come philandering down here, hoping to see the Professor? Jo, I'm ashamed of you! No, you shall not go there to borrow an umbrella or find out where he is from his friends. If you catch your death and ruin your bonnet, it's no more than you deserve. Now then!"

With that she rushed across the street so abruptly that she narrowly escaped being struck by a passing truck, and ran into the arms of a stately old gentleman who said, "I beg pardon, ma'am" and looked mortally offended. Somewhat daunted, Jo righted herself, spread her handkerchief over the ribbons, and hurried on, with increasing dampness about the ankles and much clashing of umbrellas overhead. That a somewhat dilapidated blue one remained above her unprotected bonnet attracted her attention, and looking up she saw Mr. Bhaer looking down.

"I feel to know the strong-minded lady who goes so bravely under many horse noses, and so fast through much mud. What do you down here, my friend?"

"I'm shopping."

Mr. Bhaer smiled, as he glanced from the pickle factory on one side to the wholesale hide and leather concern on the other, but he only said politely, "You haf no umbrella. May I go also, and take for you the bundles?"

"Yes, thank you."

Jo's cheeks were as red as her ribbon, and she wondered what he thought of her. But she didn't care, for in a minute she found herself walking away arm in arm with her Professor, feeling as if the sun had suddenly burst out with uncommon brilliancy, that the world was all right again, and that one thoroughly happy woman was paddling through the wet that day.

"We thought you had gone," said Jo hastily, for she knew he was looking at her.

"Did you believe that I should go with no farewell to those who had been so heavenly kind to me?"

He asked so reproachfully that she felt as if she had insulted him, and answered heartily, "No, I didn't. I knew you were busy about your own affairs, but we missed you—Father and Mother especially."

"And you?"

"I'm always glad to see you, sir."

In her anxiety to keep her voice calm, Jo made it rather cool, and the frosty little word at the end seemed to chill the Professor, for his smile vanished as he said gravely, "I thank you, and come one time more before I go."

"You are going, then?"

"I haf no longer any business here—it is done."

"Successfully, I hope?" said Jo, for he sounded disappointed.

"I ought to think so, for I had a way opened to me by which I can make my bread and gif my boys much help."

"Tell me, please! I like to know all about the boys," said Jo eagerly.

"That is so kind, I gladly tell you. My friends find for me a place in a college where I teach as at home and earn enough to make the way smooth for Franz and Emil. For this I should be grateful, should I not?"

"Indeed you should. How splendid it will be to have you doing what you like, and be able to see you often, and the boys!"cried Jo.

"Ah! But we shall not meet often, I fear. This place is at the West."

"So far away!" And Jo left her skirts to their fate, as if it didn't matter now what became of her clothes or herself.

Mr. Bhaer could read several languages, but he had not learned to read women yet. He flattered himself that he knew Jo pretty well, and was, therefore, much amazed by the contradictions of voice, face, and manner, which she showed him in rapid succession that day.

"Here's the place for my errands. Will you come in? It won't take long."

Jo prided herself upon her shopping capabilities, and particularly wished to impress her escort with the neatness and dispatch with which she would accomplish the business. But owing to the flutter she was in, everything went amiss. She upset the tray of needles, forgot the fabric was to be "twilled" till it was cut off, gave the wrong change, and covered herself with confusion by asking for lavender ribbon at the calico counter. Mr. Bhaer stood by, watching her blush and blunder.

When they came out, he put the parcel under his arm with a more cheerful aspect and splashed through the puddles as if he enjoyed it.

"Should we not do a little what you call shopping for the babies, and haf a farewell party tonight if I go for my last call at your so pleasant home?" he asked, stopping before a window full of fruit and flowers.

"What will we buy?" said Jo, ignoring the latter part of his speech.

"May they haf oranges and figs?" asked Mr. Bhaer, with a paternal air.

"They eat them when they can get them."

"Do you care for nuts?"

"Like a squirrel."

Mr. Bhaer finished the shopping by buying several pounds of expensive grapes, a pot of rosy daisies, and a pretty jar of honey. Then, distorting his pockets with the bundles and giving her the flowers to hold, he put up the old umbrella, and they traveled on again.

"Miss Marsch, I had a great favor to ask of you," began the Professor, after they had walked half a block.

"Yes, sir." Jo's heart began to beat so hard she was afraid he would hear it.

"I am bold to say it in spite of the rain, because so short a time remains to me."

"Yes, sir." And Jo nearly crushed the small flowerpot with the sudden squeeze she gave it.

"I wish to get a little dress for my Tina. Will you kindly help?"

"Yes, sir." And Jo felt as calm and cool all of a sudden as if she had stepped into a refrigerator.

"Perhaps also a shawl for Tina's mother, she is so poor and sick. Yes, yes, a thick, warm shawl would be a friendly thing to take her."

"I'll do it with pleasure, Mr. Bhaer." He's getting dearer every minute, added Jo to herself. She chose a pretty gown for Tina, and then asked to see the shawls.

"Your lady may prefer this. It's a superior article, a most desirable color, chaste and genteel," the clerk said, shaking out a comfortable gray shawl and throwing it over Jo's shoulders. He obviously thought the two were man and wife.

"Does this suit you, Mr. Bhaer?" she asked, turning her back to him and feeling deeply grateful for the chance to hide her hot face.

"Excellently well, we will haf it," answered the Professor, smiling to himself as he paid for it, while Jo continued to rummage the counters like a confirmed bargain-hunter so she wouldn't have to look at him.

"Now shall we go home?" he asked, as if the words were pleasant to him.

"Yes, it's late, and I'm so tired." Jo's voice was more pathetic than she knew, for now the sun seemed to have gone away as suddenly as it came out. The world grew muddy and miserable again, and she discovered that her feet were cold, but her heart was colder—her head ached, but her heart ached more. Mr. Bhaer was going away, he only cared for her as a friend, it was all a mistake, and the sooner it was over the better. With this idea in her head, she hailed an approaching bus with such a hasty gesture that the daisies flew out of the pot and were badly damaged.

"This is not our boos," said the Professor, waving the loaded vehicle away, and stopping to pick up the poor little flowers.

"I beg your pardon, I didn't see the name distinctly. Never mind, I can walk. I'm used to plodding in the mud," returned Jo, blinking hard, because she would have died rather than openly wipe her eyes.

Mr. Bhaer saw the drops on her cheeks, though she turned her head away. Suddenly stooping down, he asked in a tone that meant a great deal, "Heart's dearest, why do you cry?"

Now if Jo had not been new to this sort of thing, she would have said she wasn't crying and had a cold in her head. Instead, that undignified creature answered, with an irrepressible sob, "Because you are going away."

"*Ach, mein Gott*, that is so goot!" cried Mr. Bhaer, managing to clasp his hands in spite of the umbrella and the bundles. "Jo, I had nothing but much love to gif you, and I waited to be sure that I was something more than a friend. Am I? Can you make a little place in your heart for old Fritz?" he added, all in one breath.

"Oh, yes!" said Jo, and he was satisfied, for she folded both hands over his arm and looked up at him with an expression that plainly showed how happy she would be to walk through life beside him, even if she had no better shelter than his old umbrella.

It was certainly proposing under difficulties, for even if he had desired to do so, Mr. Bhaer could not go down upon his knees, on account of the mud. The only way in which he could express his rapture was to look at her with an expression which glorified his face to such a degree that there actually seemed to be little rainbows in the drops that sparkled on his beard. If he had not loved Jo, I don't think

Jo . . . plainly showed how happy she would be to walk through life beside him, even if she had no better shelter than his old umbrella.

he could have done it then, for she looked far from lovely, with her skirts in a deplorable state, her rubber boots splashed to the ankle, and her bonnet a ruin. Fortunately, Mr. Bhaer considered her the most beautiful woman living. His own hatbrim was limp with the little rills trickling upon his shoulders (for he held the umbrella all over Jo), and every finger of his gloves needed mending.

Passers-by probably thought them a pair of harmless lunatics, for they entirely forgot to hail a bus, and strolled leisurely along, oblivious of deepening dusk and fog. Little they cared what anybody thought, for they were enjoying the magical moment which bestows youth on the old, beauty on the plain, wealth on the poor, and gives human hearts a foretaste of heaven.

"Friedrich, why didn't you . . ."

"Ah, she gifs me the name that no one speaks since Minna died!" cried the Professor, pausing in a puddle to regard her with grateful delight.

"I won't, unless you like it."

"Like it? It is more sweet to me than I can tell."

"Well, then, why didn't you tell me all this sooner?" asked Jo bashfully.

"Now I shall haf to show you all my heart, and I so gladly will, because you must take care of it hereafter. See, then, my Jo—ah, the dear, funny little name!—I had a wish to tell something the day I said goodbye in New York, but I thought the handsome friend was betrothed to you, and so I spoke not. Would you have said yes then if I had spoken?"

"I don't know. I'm afraid not, for I didn't have any heart just then."

"I haf waited so long, I am grown selfish, as you will find, Professorin."

"I like that," cried Jo, delighted with her new name. "Now tell me what brought you, at last, just when I most wanted you?"

"This." And Mr. Bhaer took a little worn paper out of his waistcoat pocket.

Jo unfolded it and looked much abashed, for it was one of her own contributions to a paper that paid for poetry, which accounted for her sending it an occasional attempt.

"How could that bring you?" she asked, wondering what he meant.

"I found it by chance. I knew it by the names and the initials, and in it there was one little verse that seemed to call me. Read."

Jo obeyed, and hastily skimmed through the lines which she had christened

IN THE GARRETT

Four little chests, all in a row,
    Dim with dust, and worn by time,
All fashioned and filled, long ago,
    By children now in their prime.
Four little keys hung side by side,
    With faded ribbons, brave and gay
When fastened their with childish pride,
    Long ago on a rainy day.

"Meg" on the first lid, smooth and fair.
    I look in with loving eyes,
For folded here, with well-known care,
    A goodly gathering lies.
Ah, happy mother! well I know
    You hear, like a sweet refrain,
Lullabies ever soft and low
    In the falling summer rain.

"Jo" on the next lid, scratched and worn,
    And within a motley store
Of headless dolls, of schoolbooks torn,
    Birds and beasts that speak no more.
A woman in a lonely home,
    Hearing, like a sad refrain—

"Be worthy love, and love will come,"
  In the falling summer rain.

My Beth! the dust is always swept
  From the lid that bears your name,
As if by loving eyes that wept,
  By careful hands that often came.
The songs she sang, without lament,
  In her prison-house of pain,
Forever are they sweetly blent
  With the falling summer rain.

Upon the last lid's polished field—
  Legend now both fair and true
A gallant knight bears on his shield,
  "Amy" in letters gold and blue.
Now learning fairer, truer spells,
  Hearing, like a blithe refrain,
The silver sound of wedding bells
  In the falling summer rain.

 Four little chests all in a row,
  Dim with dust, and worn by time,
Four women, taught by weal and woe
  To love and labor in their prime.
Lives whose brave music long shall ring
  Like a spirit-stirring strain,
Souls that shall gladly soar and sing
  In the long sunshine after rain.

                    J.M.

"It's bad poetry, but I felt it when I wrote it, one day when I was lonely, and had a good cry. I never thought it would go where it could tell tales," said Jo, tearing up the verses the Professor had treasured so long.

"Let it go. It has done its duty, and I will haf a fresh one when I read all the brown book in which she keeps her little secrets," said Mr. Bhaer with a smile as he watched the fragments fly away on the wind. "Yes," he added earnestly, "I read that, and I think to myself, She has a sorrow, she is lonely. I haf a heart full, full for her. Shall I not go and say, 'If this is not too poor a thing, take it in Gott's name?' "

"And so you came to find that it was not too poor, but the one precious thing I needed," whispered Jo.

"I had no courage to think that at first, heavenly kind as was your welcome to me. But soon I began to hope, and then I said, 'I will haf her if I die for it,' and so I will!" cried Mr. Bhaer, with a defiant nod.

Jo thought that was splendid, and resolved to be worthy of her knight.

"What made you stay away so long?" she asked presently.

"It was not easy, but I could not find the heart to take you from that so happy home for a poor old fellow!"

"I'm glad you are poor. I couldn't bear a rich husband," said Jo decidedly, adding in a softer tone, "And don't call yourself old—forty is the prime of life. I couldn't help loving you if you were seventy! I'll carry my share, Friedrich, and help to support the home. Make up your mind to that, or I'll never go."

"We shall see. Haf you patience to wait a long time, Jo? I must help my boys first, because, even for you, I may not break my word to Minna. Can you forgif that, and be happy while we hope and wait?"

"Yes, I know I can, for we love one another. I have my duty, also, and my work. I couldn't enjoy myself if I neglected them. You can do your part out West, I can do mine here, and both be happy hoping for the best, and leaving the future to be as God wills."

"Ah! You gif me such hope and courage, and I haf nothing to gif back but a full heart and these empty hands," cried the Professor, overcome.

Jo would never learn to be proper, for as they stood upon the steps, she put both hands into his, whispering tenderly, "Not empty now," and kissed her Friedrich under the umbrella. It was daring, but she would have done it even if the flock of draggle-tailed sparrows on the hedge had been humans watching. That was the crowning moment of both their lives, when, turning from the night and cold and loneliness to the household light and warmth and peace waiting to receive them, with a glad "Welcome home!" Jo led her lover in, and shut the door.

24
HARVEST TIME

FOR A YEAR JO AND HER PROFESSOR worked and waited, met occasionally, and wrote such long letters that according to Laurie they alone accounted for the rising price of paper. The second year began sadly, for Aunt March died. But when their first sorrow was over—for they loved the old lady in spite of her sharp tongue—they found they had cause for rejoicing, for she had left Plumfield to Jo, which made all sorts of joyful things possible.

"It's a fine old place and will bring a handsome sum, for of course you intend to sell it," said Laurie, as they were all talking the matter over some weeks later.

"No, I don't," was Jo's firm answer, as she petted the fat poodle, whom she had adopted out of respect to his former owner.

"You don't mean to live there?"

"Yes, I do."

"But, my dear girl, it's an immense house and will take a power of money to keep it in order. The garden and orchard alone need two or three men, and farming isn't in Bhaer's line, I take it."

"He'll try his hand at it there, if I propose it."

"And you expect to live off the land? Well, that sounds like paradise, but you'll find it desperate hard work."

"The crop we are going to raise is a profitable one." And Jo laughed.

"Of what is this fine crop to consist, ma'am?"

"Boys. I want to open a school for little lads—a good, happy, home-like school, with me to take care of them and Fritz to teach them."

"Isn't that just like her?" cried Laurie, appealing to the family, who looked as much surprised as he.

"I like it," said Mrs. March decidedly.

"So do I," added her husband, who welcomed the thought of a chance for trying the Socratic method of education on modern youth.

"It will be an immense care for Jo," said Meg, stroking the head of her one all-absorbing son.

"Jo can do it and be happy in it. It's a splendid idea. Tell us all about it," cried Mr. Laurence, who had been longing to lend the lovers a hand but knew they would refuse his help.

"I knew you'd stand by me, sir. Amy does too—I see it in her eyes, though she prudently waits to turn it over in her mind before she speaks. Now, my dear people," continued Jo earnestly, "just understand that this isn't a new idea of mine, but a long-cherished plan. Before my Fritz came, I used to think how, when I'd made my fortune and no one needed me at home, I'd hire a big house and pick up some poor, forlorn little lads who hadn't any mothers and take care of them and make life jolly for them before it was too late."

Mrs. March held out her hand to Jo, who took it, smiling, with tears in her eyes, and went on in the old enthusiastic way, which they had not seen for a long while.

"I told my plan to Fritz once, and he said it was just what he would like, and agreed to try it when we got rich. Bless his dear heart, money doesn't stay in his pocket long enough to lay up any. But now, thanks to my good old aunt, who loved me better than I ever deserved, I'm rich—at least I feel so—and we can live at Plumfield perfectly well, if we have a flourishing school. It's just the place for boys—there's plenty of room for dozens inside and splendid grounds

211

outside. They could help in the garden and orchard—such work is healthy, isn't it, sir? Then Fritz can train and teach in his own way, and Father will help him. Think what luxury! Plumfield my own and a wilderness of boys to enjoy it with me!"

As Jo waved her hands and gave a sigh of rapture, the family went off into a gale of merriment, and Mr. Laurence laughed till they thought he'd have a fit.

"I don't see anything funny," she said gravely, when she could be heard. "Nothing could be more natural or proper than for my Professor to open a school and for me to prefer to reside on my own estate."

"She is putting on airs already," said Laurie, who regarded the idea as a great joke. "But may I inquire how you intend to support the establishment?

"Now don't be a wet-blanket, Teddy. Of course I shall have rich pupils, also—perhaps begin with such altogether. Then when I've got a start, I can take a ragamuffin or two, just for a relish. Rich people's children often need care and comfort, as well as poor. Some are naughty through mismanagement or neglect, and some lose their mothers. Besides, the best have to get through the hobbledehoy age, and that's the very time they need most patience and kindness. People hustle them about, try to keep them out of sight, and expect them to turn all at once from pretty children into fine young men. They don't complain much—plucky little souls—but they feel it. I've a special interest in such young bears and like to show them that I see the warm, honest, well-meaning boys' hearts, in spite of the clumsy arms and legs and the topsy-turvy heads. I've had experience, too, for haven't I brought up one boy to be a pride and honor to his family?"

"I'll testify that you tried to do it," said Laurie with a grateful look.

"And I've succeeded beyond my hopes. For here you are, a steady, sensible businessman, doing heaps of good with your money, and laying up the blessings of the poor instead of dollars. But you are not merely a businessman—you love good and beautiful things. I am proud of you, Teddy, for you get better every year, and everyone feels it. Yes, I'll just point to you and say, 'There's your model, my lads.' "

"I say, Jo, that's too much," Laurie began, in his old boyish way. "You have all done more for me than I can ever thank you for, except by doing my best not to disappoint you. You have rather cast me off lately, Jo, so if I've got on at all, you may thank these two for it." And he laid one hand gently on his grandfather's white head, the other on Amy's golden one, for the three were never far apart.

"I do think that families are the most beautiful things in all the world!" burst out Jo, who was in an unusually uplifted frame of mind just then. "When I have one of my own, I hope it will be as happy as the three I know and love the best." And that night when she went to her room after a blissful evening of family counsels, hopes, and plans, her heart was so full of happiness that she could only calm it by kneeling beside the empty bed always near her own, and thinking tender thoughts of Beth.

Almost before she knew where she was, Jo found herself married and settled at Plumfield. Then a family of six or seven boys sprung up like mushrooms, and flourished surprisingly, poor boys as well as rich. Mr. Laurence was continually finding some poor boy and begging the Bhaers to take pity on the child, and he would gladly pay a trifle for its support. In this way the sly old gentleman furnished proud Jo with the style of boy in which she most delighted.

How Jo did enjoy her "wilderness of boys," and how poor, dear Aunt March would have lamented had she been there to see the sacred precincts of prim, well-ordered Plumfield overrun with Toms, Dicks, and Harrys! It never was a fashionable school, and the Professor did not lay up a fortune. But it was just what Jo intended it to be: "a happy, homelike place for boys who needed teaching, care, and kindness." Every room in the big house was soon full and every little plot in the garden soon had its owner. A regular menagerie appeared in barn and shed, for pet animals were allowed. Three times a day, Jo smiled at her Fritz from the head of a long table lined on either side with rows of happy young faces, which all turned to her with affectionate eyes, confiding words, and hearts full of love for "Mother Bhaer."

They were not angels, by any means, and some of them caused both Professor and Professorin much trouble and anxiety. But her faith in the good spot which exists in the heart of the naughtiest little ragamuffin gave her patience, skill, and in time success, for no mortal boy could hold out long with Father Bhaer shining on him as benevolently as the sun and Mother Bhaer forgiving him seventy times seven. There were slow boys and bashful boys, feeble boys and riotous boys, boys that stuttered and boys that were lame, and a merry little mixed-race boy, who was welcome though some people predicted that his admission would ruin the school.

Yes, Jo was a happy woman there in spite of hard work, much anxiety, and a perpetual racket. As the years went on, two little sons of her own came to increase her happiness—Rob, named for Grandpa, and Teddy, a happy-go-lucky baby, who seemed to have inherited his papa's sunshiny temper as well as his mother's lively spirit. How they ever grew up alive in that whirlpool of boys was a mystery to their grandma and aunts, but they flourished like dandelions in spring.

There were a great many holidays at Plumfield, and one of the most delightful was the yearly apple-picking; for then the Marches, Laurences, Brookes, and Bhaers turned out in full force and made a day of it. Five years after Jo's wedding, one of these fruitful festivals occurred—a mellow October day, when the air was full of an exhilarating freshness which made the spirits rise and the blood dance. The old orchard wore its holiday attire, and every tree stood ready to send down its shower of red or yellow apples at the first shake. Everybody was there. Everybody laughed and sang. Everybody declared there never had been such a perfect day.

At four o'clock the apple-pickers rested and compared bruises.

Then Jo and Meg, with a detachment of the bigger boys, set forth the supper on the grass, for an outdoor tea was always the crowning joy of the day. Some boys tried the pleasing experiment of drinking milk while standing on their heads, others lent a charm to leapfrog by eating pie, cookies were all over the field, and apple turnovers roosted in the trees like a new style of bird. The little girls had a private tea party, and Ted roamed among the edibles at his own sweet will.

When no one could eat any more, the Professor announced as usual: "Aunt March, God bless her!" He never forgot how much he owed her and taught the boys to remember the woman who gave them Plumfield.

"Now, Grandma's sixtieth birthday! Long life to her, with three cheers!"

The cheering, once begun, was hard to stop. Everybody's health was cheered, from Mr. Laurence to the astonished guinea pig who had strayed into the party. Demi, as the oldest grandchild, then presented the queen of the day with various gifts, so numerous that they were transported to the festive scene in a wheelbarrow. The children's gifts were all their own. Every stitch Daisy's patient little fingers had put into the handkerchiefs she hemmed was better than embroidery to Mrs. March. Demi's shoebox was a miracle of mechanical skill, though the cover wouldn't shut. Rob's footstool had a wiggle in its uneven legs that she declared was soothing. No page of the costly book Amy's child gave her was so fair as that on which appeared, in tipsy capitals, the words, "To dear Grandma, from her little Beth."

During this ceremony the boys had mysteriously disappeared, and when Mrs. March had tearfully tried to thank her children, the Professor suddenly began to sing. Then, from above him, voice after voice took up the words, and from tree to tree echoed the music of the unseen choir, as the boys sang with all their hearts the little song Jo had written and Laurie had set to music. Mrs. March couldn't get over her surprise and insisted on shaking hands with every one of the featherless birds.

After this, the boys went back to their fun, leaving Mrs. March and her daughters under the festival tree.

"I don't think I ever ought to call myself 'Unlucky Jo' again, when my greatest wish has come true so beautifully," said Mrs. Bhaer, taking Teddy's little fist out of the milk pitcher, in which he was happily churning.

"And yet your life is different from the one you pictured. Do you remember our castles in the air?" asked Amy, smiling as she watched Laurie and John playing cricket with the boys.

"Dear fellows! It does my heart good to see them forget business and frolic for a day," answered Jo, who now spoke in a maternal way of all mankind. "Yes, I remember. But the life I wanted then seems selfish and cold to me now. I haven't given up the hope that I may write a good book yet, but I can wait. I'm sure it will be all the better for these experiences." And Jo pointed from the boys in the distance to her father, leaning on the Professor's arm, as they walked to and fro in the sunshine, deep in one of the conversations which both enjoyed so much—and then to her mother, sitting enthroned among her daughters with grandchildren.

"I asked for splendid things, to be sure, but in my heart I knew I should be satisfied if I had a little home and John and some dear children. I've got them all, thank God, and am the happiest woman in the world." And Meg laid her hand on her tall boy's head, with a face full of tender contentment.

"My castle is very different from what I planned, but I would not alter it, though, like Jo, I don't relinquish all my artistic hopes. I've begun to model a figure of baby, and Laurie says it is the best thing I've ever done. I think so myself, and mean to do it in marble, so that whatever happens, I may at least keep the image of my little angel."

As Amy spoke, a great tear dropped on the golden hair of the sleeping child in her arms, for her one well-beloved daughter was a frail little creature and the dread of losing her was the shadow over Amy's sunshine.

Amy's nature was growing sweeter, deeper, and more tender. Laurie was growing more serious, strong, and firm. Both were learning that beauty, youth, good fortune, even love itself, cannot keep care and pain, loss and sorrow, from the most blessed.

"She is growing better, I am sure of it, my dear. Don't despair, but hope and keep happy," said Mrs. March, as tenderhearted Daisy lay her rosy cheek against her little cousin's pale one.

"I never ought to, while I have you to cheer me up, Marmee, and Laurie to take more than half of every burden," replied Amy warmly. "He is so sweet and patient with me, so devoted to Beth, that I can't love him enough. So, in spite of my one cross, I can say with Meg, 'Thank God, I'm a happy woman.' "

"There's no need for me to say it, for everyone can see that I'm far happier than I deserve," added Jo, glancing from her good husband to her chubby children, tumbling on the grass beside her. "Fritz is getting gray and stout; I'm growing as thin as a shadow, and am thirty; we never shall be rich. But in spite of these unromantic facts, I have nothing to complain of and never was so jolly in my life."

"Yes, Jo, I think your harvest will be a good one," began Mrs. March, frightening away a big black cricket.

"Not half so good as yours, Mother. Here it is, and we never can thank you enough for the patient sowing and reaping you have done."

"I hope there will be more wheat and fewer tares every year," said Amy softly.

"A large sheaf, but I know there's room in your heart for it, Marmee dear," added Meg's tender voice.

Touched to the heart, Mrs. March could only stretch out her arms, as if to gather children and grandchildren to herself, and say, with face and voice full of motherly love, gratitude, and humility, "Oh, my girls, however long you may live, I never can wish you a greater happiness than this!"